Tucking Adele into his side, Brian placed his hand on his weapon.

"Back inside—now."

The driver's side window lowered, a black muzzle appeared and the driver fired. The loud retort echoed off the stone walls. Adele gasped. Heart jolting, Brian shoved her toward the safety of the glass doors and was gratified she didn't hesitate to run.

Pulling his weapon free, Brian returned fire, hitting the sedan and shattering the front windshield. The car reversed, spun 180 degrees, swiping the end of a luxury coupe, and shot forward, disappearing as it sped out of the parking garage.

"Brian?"

He turned to find Adele standing in the hospital doorway, her topaz eyes wide with shock.

Moving swiftly to her side, he ushered her farther into the hospital. She trembled beneath his hand.

"What was that?" she asked.

"Someone tried to kill you. Again."

Terri Reed's romance and romantic suspense novels have appeared on the *Publishers Weekly* top twenty-five and NPD BookScan top one hundred lists and have been featured in *USA TODAY*, *Christian Fiction* magazine and *RT Book Reviews*. Her books have been finalists for the Romance Writers of America RITA® Award and the National Readers' Choice Award and finalists three times for the American Christian Fiction Writers Carol Award. Contact Terri at terrireed.com or PO Box 19555, Portland, OR 97224.

Books by Terri Reed

Love Inspired Suspense

Buried Mountain Secrets
Secret Mountain Hideout
Christmas Protection Detail
Secret Sabotage
Forced to Flee
Forced to Hide

Rocky Mountain K-9 Unit

Detection Detail

Alaska K-9 Unit

Alaskan Rescue

True Blue K-9 Unit: Brooklyn

Explosive Situation

True Blue K-9 Unit

Seeking the Truth

Visit the Author Profile page at LoveInspired.com for more titles.

FORCED TO HIDE

TERRI REED

LOVE INSPIRED SUSPENSE
INSPIRATIONAL ROMANCE

LOVE INSPIRED SUSPENSE
INSPIRATIONAL ROMANCE

ISBN-13: 978-1-335-58824-1

Forced to Hide

Copyright © 2023 by Terri Reed

For questions and comments about the quality of this book, please contact us at CustomerService@Harlequin.com.

Love Inspired
22 Adelaide St. West, 41st Floor
Toronto, Ontario M5H 4E3, Canada
www.LoveInspired.com

Printed in U.S.A.

In God I will praise his word, in God I have put my trust;
I will not fear what flesh can do unto me.
—*Psalm* 56:4

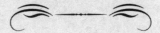

To my son—you are a joy, a man of honor and integrity.
I love you.

ONE

"All rise." The bailiff's voice rang clear through the high ceilings of the courtroom and bounced off the wood paneling. "The federal district court of the great State of Texas is in session. The Honorable Judge Adele Weston presiding."

Adele hesitated a fraction of a second before entering the courtroom through the open doorway of the judge's chamber. A ripple of disquiet cascaded through her limbs at the barely perceptible sound of crinkling paper.

The parole hearing notice she'd stuffed into the pocket of her judge's robe weighed her down. She smoothed a hand over her black robe and took a breath. The scent of wood polish teased the air. She rolled her shoulders, putting the past out of her mind. At least for now.

She needed to be fully present to do her job.

After two years of sitting on the federal district court bench in her home state, she still battled nerves every time she entered the court-room. But she couldn't predict when something, like the piece of mail she'd opened earlier, might trigger the panic lurking at the edges of her consciousness.

Gathering her bravado, she let out her breath, squared her shoulders and strode forward.

You can do this. The mantra played on repeat through her brain. *You are strong.*

She smiled and nodded to Harry Calvin, the court bailiff, as she passed him. Harry's stoic expression didn't crack. The older officer took his job as court guard seriously, and his pres-ence steadied her nerves. She was safe here within the domain of the courthouse.

Her judicial assistant, Jordan Umi, fresh out of college and eager to please, gave her a nod as he took his seat off to the left side of the bench. The court reporter, Rachel Brown, sat in front of the bench.

Taking comfort in the familiar tableau, Adele stepped up to the dais, her gaze sweeping over the sea of faces staring at her.

Up front was the federal prosecutor and his two clerks sitting at the table to the left, while on the right was the criminal defense attorney, her two clerks and the defendant, Tomas Garcia.

The gallery teemed with potential jurors and the US marshal detail assigned to guard and keep track of the man whose fate would be in the hands of twelve men and women.

Several months ago, the US Marshals Service managed to bring down the head of a vicious drug cartel operating in Texas. Today's proceedings started the process of giving Mr. Garcia his day in court.

"You may be seated." Adele enunciated each syllable in a clear voice, thankful her earlier tension had dissipated.

She took her own seat and scooted the chair forward, her knee bumping up against something hard underneath the desk. Aware of all the gazes intently staring at her, she ignored the stinging sensation and silently lamented the bruise no doubt already forming. She made a mental note to have maintenance inspect the bench after the session. The courthouse and its furnishings were old and in need of updating. Apparently, the bench was falling apart.

Adjusting the microphone, her gaze once again brushed over the potential jurors. Men and women of varying ages and ethnicities stared back at her with expressions ranging from boredom to curiosity.

"Good morning, ladies and gentlemen," Adele intoned with slow and deliberate intention. "Thank you all for doing your civic duty and responding to your jury summons. This is a sacred responsibility of participation, and we couldn't function in our system without the assistance of people like yourselves."

She shifted in her seat, her knee hitting the hard object and causing her to jerk away from the offending article, the sound of ripping fabric echoing in her ears. Irritation swamped her. "Excuse me a moment."

She pushed the chair back from the bench and dipped her head to look underneath. Within the dark cavernous space, blinking lights assaulted her. She could make out the shape of something square with sharp edges attached to the side of the bench. Her mind scrambled to make sense of what she was seeing.

An explosive device?

Her breath froze in her lungs.

Please, God, no!

She jumped out of her seat. A murmur of confusion rippled through the room. She needed to get everyone out of the courtroom. Her heart hammered against her ribs and her blood pounded in her veins.

Not wanting to start a panicked riot, she turned to Harry and said as calmly as she could in a low voice, "We need to evacuate. Now."

She gestured to the space beneath the bench.

Harry frowned and ducked his head to see what she pointed at. His stoic demeanor faltered. He moved swiftly to the wall behind the bench and pulled the fire alarm. The shrill sound filled the air and bounced off the paneling. So much for not causing a panic.

Adele waved her arms and urged, "Go. Go!"

The US marshals grabbed their charge and swiftly ushered him out. The potential selection of jurors fled through the back doors behind the marshals. The lawyers and their clerks pushed after them.

Harry bound up the steps, grabbing her by the arm. The feel of his hand wrapped around her biceps shuddered through her.

"But we have to make sure everyone gets to safety," she protested as he propelled her away from the bench, her head swiveling to find Jordan. The young man hurried after them.

Just as the bailiff tugged her through the doorway into the judge's chamber, the bomb attached to the underside of the bench exploded.

Adele could only gasp as the force of the blast sent her stumbling forward, like a hard shove from behind. The deafening noise rang in her ears. Another set of explosions took her to the ground with jarring impact. She covered her head with her hands as debris rained down like blows.

For a blinding moment, she was transported back to a dark alley and the foul stench of sweat and blood filling her senses. The carpeted floor absorbed her scream.

A distant explosion rocked through the US Marshals Service building. Within seconds, the ringing of phones throughout the service headquarters sent a shiver of dread down US deputy marshal Brian Forrester's spine.

The office door at the end of the bullpen opened and the US marshal for the Western District of Texas, Gavin Armstrong, hustled out.

From the dire expression on the boss's face, Brian feared something bad had happened.

"The federal district courthouse has been bombed."

Definitely bad.

"The Garcia trial…" Deputy Jace Armstrong said from his temporary desk. Jace no longer lived or worked out of Texas, having moved to Oregon to be with his new bride. But because the trial was starting, he'd returned to be here to testify and to be on hand to make sure nothing derailed the case against Tomas Garcia.

"The jury selection courtroom was the target," Gavin stated.

A stone dropped in Brian's stomach. "An assassination attempt on Garcia?" Many people wanted Tomas Garcia dead. The man had a long legacy of violence.

"Could be whomever is taking over his organization wants him eliminated," Deputy Seraphina Morales said. "Just because we have Tomas Garcia in custody doesn't mean his operation is disabled."

Jace spun to stare at her. "Both Tomas and his son, Marco, are out of the picture. We've arrested all the top lieutenants. There's no one left to take over."

The thread of concern in his buddy's tone wasn't lost on Brian. Several months ago, Tomas Garcia had tried to kidnap an innocent woman, the daughter of a man who had witnessed Tomas's son, Marco Garcia, commit murder. Jace had been tasked with keeping the woman, Abby Frost, safe and, in the process, had fallen in love with Abby while protecting her from the Garcias. Brian and Sera had helped in the takedown of the Garcia cartel.

"Maybe. Or maybe not," Sera said. "I've been tracking drug overdoses and arrests since we apprehended Garcia. There was a gap for a short time, but activity has been going up again."

"A rival cartel muscling in?" Jace suggested.

It wasn't unusual for other drug lords to assume control of a crippled competitor.

"Gear up," Gavin said. "We have to secure the judge and the prosecutor. Garcia's detail has him already en route to the hospital. I'm not clear on the extent of his injuries."

As the four of them hurried to the armory, along with every other marshal at headquarters, Brian asked, "Who's the presiding judge?"

"Adele Weston."

Brian's steps faltered and his heart gave a giant thud as the image of beautiful topaz-colored eyes flashed through his mind. "Is she hurt?"

"I don't have the statistics on any fatalities or injured beyond Garcia and his guard detail," Gavin replied, donning a flak vest.

Reining in the crushing sense of doom, Brian put on his own vest, checked his weapons and grabbed extra magazine clips.

"EOD is on the way," Gavin said, referring to the explosive ordinance detection team. "When we get there, we have to wait for them to clear the building before we can move in."

"We should check the gawkers," Jace said. "See if the bomber's watching the chaos."

"Good idea," Gavin said. "You and Sera work the scene. Brian, you secure the judge."

"No," Brian stated before he could stop himself.

All eyes turned to him.

He cringed. Challenging his boss wasn't a smart move.

"If what Sera suspects is true, that the cartel is up and running again, things are going to get real lively real fast. Especially if the attack on the courthouse is cartel related," Brian stated. "I'd be more effective…"

Gavin held up a hand. "The judge."

The firm tone brooked no argument. Brian stifled a resigned sigh.

"You want to share the reason you don't want to protect the judge?" Jace asked with a sideways glance as they filed out the US marshals' headquarters' back door.

Gut churning with dread, Brian said, "No reason."

"Right."

Jace's disbelieving tone had Brian wincing. His friend knew him too well.

Brian kept his mouth closed. No way was he going to admit he'd once asked Judge Weston out and had been soundly turned down.

The assaulting noise of the fire alarm had ceased but the overhead sprinkler system had kicked in, spraying water everywhere, soaking Adele as she lay sprawled on her belly on the floor. Her robe clung to her back. Water dripped into her eyes. She rolled to the side, shielding her face from the spray.

A hand gripped Adele's shoulder. She jerked away, flinching from the touch.

"Ma'am, are you okay?"

The bailiff's voice sounded muffled to her, like she had cotton in her ears.

Breathing deep to push back the memories that taunted her, she nodded and sat up. Various spots of her body protested the movement. She gripped Harry's forearm. "I'm fine. You?"

The older man straightened with a nod.

"Jordan?" Adele pushed to her knees, her gaze searching for her court clerk. He'd been behind them. Though the air was hazy with smoke, debris and steaming water, she could make out Jordan's prone figure lying just inside the judge's chamber doorway.

She crawled over to him.

Harry followed her. "He okay?"

She checked Jordan's neck for a pulse. The faint flutter beneath her fingertips had her dropping her head in relief. "He's alive." She turned to Harry. "We need to get paramedics here."

Pushing to her feet, she wobbled as the world tilted. She grabbed onto the doorframe. "We have to check on the others."

Harry gripped her arm. "No, ma'am. You're injured. You need to sit back down."

Allowing the bailiff to urge her away from the doorway and to the rose-colored Victorian couch that sat against the wall beneath her framed diplomas and various pictures chronicling her career, she sank onto the cushioned seat.

Through the fuzziness in her ear, she heard ringing. She tugged at her earlobe, thinking the noise was inside her head then realized it was her cell phone. She started to rise, but Harry wagged his finger at her.

"You stay put."

"My purse, Harry. In my desk drawer."

With a sharp nod, the older man turned and

stumbled to her desk, barely catching himself by gripping the edge and staying upright.

"Harry! You're hurt." Adele slowly rose from the couch to keep from losing her own balance. When she had her bearings, she hurried across the room and pushed Harry into the captain's chair behind her desk.

"Don't worry about me, ma'am," Harry told her. "I'm as sturdy as a tree."

"Even trees fall down." She opened her desk drawer and dug through her purse for her phone. It had stopped ringing. But she had ten missed calls. Her sister, her mother, her father, her friends and Senator Ortega. She grimaced. "Phone lines must be out."

Two paramedics came through the door, one making a beeline for her.

She shook her head and gestured to Harry and Jordan. "These two need to be taken care of before me. I'm fine."

"We'll see about that," a deep masculine voice said from behind her.

A strange shiver raced along her limbs and she spun around to find herself face-to-face with US deputy marshal Brian Forrester.

Of course. The marshals service would take control of her safety. But him?

Her brain fritzed. Every cell in her body

jangled and clamored to attention. She'd met him over two years ago at a charity function in downtown San Antonio, though saying they'd met was a stretch. She'd just been appointed to her judgeship and had been riding on a career high when, out of the blue, he'd approached her during a lull in the event.

But if she was honest, she had noted him earlier in the evening. He was hard to miss. Taller than most everyone else in the room, with a head of tasseled blond hair and striking green eyes, he'd had every female at the charity auction paying attention. She'd tried to keep her interest in check, but then he'd appeared at her side, oozing charm, making her laugh, and then asking her out.

His attention had made her heart race. Part of her had wanted to accept but she couldn't. The thought of letting anyone get too close had sent ribbons of anxiety through her, tying her up in knots. When he'd tried coaxing her to accept, she'd turned tail and run, avoiding him the rest of the evening.

And now here he was again. Turning tail and running wasn't an option. Her heart hammered against her rib cage. She kept her lips firmly closed. She'd heard Brian had transferred to

California. What was he doing here, standing in front of her, in her chambers?

A flash of something crossed his handsome face. Confusion or irritation, she couldn't decide before he stepped forward. "Judge Weston. I'm US deputy marshal Brian Forrester." He flashed his badge at her, as if she needed the added confirmation that he was whom he claimed.

It took a moment to corral her careening senses. Did he remember asking her out? Probably not. Why would he?

When she didn't respond, Brian's dark blond brows dipped into a deep frown. He moved forward and wrapped an arm around her shoulders.

Stiffening at his touch, she ground out, "What are you doing?"

With gentle pressure, he steered her back to the couch and propelled her to take a seat "You're as pale as a cloud."

Using the radio on his utility belt, he spoke into the device. "We need another medic in the judge's chamber. The judge is hurt."

Hurt? Adele stared at him in confusion. Other than being rattled, she was fine. She had to be fine.

He knelt beside her and reached for the hem of her robe, lifting it up.

Pulse jumping, she recoiled and batted at his hands. "Excuse me?"

He sat back on his heels, concern swirling in the depths of his eyes. "Ma'am, you're injured."

She shook her head vigorously. "No, I'm not."

She started to rise. But Brian reached out a hand, braced it against her shoulder and gently kept her in place.

"Your leg is bleeding," he said softly.

Jerking her gaze from his, she stared at her leg where the robe had ripped. Blood oozed from a gash. She grimaced. He was right. But still…

His radio crackled; a disembodied voice filled the space between them. "It'll be a few minutes before we can get another paramedic back there. We have multiple injuries here."

"Casualties?" Adele asked quickly then held her breath.

His gaze never left her as he repeated her question into the radio.

He had the greenest eyes. And his hair had lightened considerably since the last time she'd seen him. She supposed that's what the California sun did. He must've been outdoors a lot. Surfing in the Pacific Ocean? The image of him on a board seared her mind.

"None. But the court reporter is in grave condition," the voice said from the radio.

The news heaved through Adele and she gasped. Tears pricked her eyes and her heart spasmed. "Rachel."

Adele lifted a silent prayer for the woman.

Sympathy darkened Brian's gaze. "Let's get you to the hospital."

"I'm not leaving." She looked past Brian's shoulder to where the paramedics worked on Jordan. "Please make sure my staff are taken care of first."

"That's not my job, ma'am," Brian told her, his voice firm. He rose, towering over her. He thumbed his radio again. "I'm bringing the judge out. Have an ambulance ready."

Outrage flamed in her cheeks. "How dare you defy an order."

Brian grinned, his whole face transforming into a beautiful vision that made her breath catch and a flush crept up her neck. *Attraction*, her rational brain acknowledged. She shoved it aside. The last thing she needed was to test her faulty judgment where men were concerned. She'd made a horrible mistake in college by trusting the wrong man. Never again.

"You're not the boss of me." Brian's tone held a note of amusement.

Taken aback, she opened her mouth, but before she could respond to his juvenile quip, he swooped in, slipping one arm around her back and the other beneath her knees, and lifted her, settling her against his chest.

She squawked, her arms going around his neck for balance. His scent, a subtle aroma of cedar and spices, teased her senses. Her breaths rattled in her chest. The need to dive away from his hold pounded at her mind, yet something kept her in place. She clung to outrage. "You can't possibly…"

"Oh, but I am," he stated firmly and proceeded to carry her out of the building.

TWO

Debris and dust floated in the air even in the back hallway, far from the courtroom where the bomb had wreaked its destruction. Brian blinked to clear his vision as he tightened his hold on the precious cargo in his arms.

Adele wasn't a small woman, nearly as tall as him, but holding her in his arms was no hardship. She smelled soft and flowery beyond the stench of the bomb. Her hands gripped the back of his neck. He'd wondered what it would be like to hold her in his arms. Never in his wildest imaginings had he thought he'd be carrying her from her judge's chamber, nor the reason why.

Who had blown up the courtroom?

Was Garcia the target? Or someone else? The judge? Brian tightened his hold on her. The prosecutor? How had they gotten the bomb inside the courtroom? It had to have been an inside job.

Anger and concern fused together in a knot, making his gut contract. During the hunt for Tomas Garcia, the marshals had discovered a deep mole within the US Marshals Service. An administrative assistant, who'd been a long-time employee, had advanced through the ranks until she'd worked directly with US marshal Gavin Armstrong.

It turned out she was a cousin of Tomas. She now sat in jail, awaiting her own trial.

The marshals had hoped she'd been the only spy. But apparently there had been another. Someone with access to the courtroom.

How had this happened? The courthouse security had vetted everyone with access to the federal buildings over the past few months, with no one standing out as a plant by the cartel. But then again, the admin assistant would have also passed if the situation hadn't gone critical and Marco, Tomas's son, hadn't blown her cover in an effort to get to Jace and Abby.

The hallway leading from her judge's chamber through the back of the courthouse was dark, save for the muted light of the emergency exit sign drawing him toward the door. He strode forward cautiously in case a chunk of the ceiling or some other debris lay on the floor. He wouldn't want to trip with the judge in his arms.

"You didn't have to carry me," Adele said, her voice infused with a good dose of irritation.

"It seemed the most prudent and expedited way to get you to the paramedics," he replied. He wasn't going to apologize for doing his job.

He hit the bar on the exit door with his hip, and they burst into the February sunlight. Though they were on the backside of the courthouse, chaos reigned.

The courthouse staff had gathered in little groups either on the back lawn or near the parking lot. He could only imagine the pandemonium at the front entrance where the jurors had fled to. He didn't envy Jace and Sera as they sorted through the mess there.

An ambulance waited twenty feet from the exit, the rear doors open and paramedics already rushing toward him. He declined their offer to take Adele from his arms and carried her to the ambulance, where he set her gently on the wide back bumper.

To the paramedics he said, "Open laceration on her right leg, possible head wound." He stepped back to allow them access.

Adele batted at the paramedics. "I'm not hurt. It's barely a scratch."

"Let us determine that," the older of the two paramedics said firmly.

A commotion behind Brian had him whirling to face the oncoming threat, his hand going to his holstered weapon. News reporters with their cameras and microphones jostled each other for prominence, their intent to get to the judge clear.

Protective instincts surged. Somewhere in the back of Brian's mind, the knowledge those instincts weren't just because of his job danced, trying to gain his attention. But he had to remain focused. He pulled in a calming breath. This woman he was protecting had nearly been blown up.

Brian stepped forward and spread out his arms, blocking the press's access. "Everyone, back off. This is an active crime scene. We don't need you interfering."

"Excuse me, let me through," a deep voice boomed over the crowd of reporters.

A man in his mid-to-late forties of medium build and height, with dark hair and dark brown eyes, pushed his way to the front. His tailored suit spoke of money, his gelled hair and shiny shoes pegged him as not part of the media. He looked vaguely familiar. Brian stepped into his path when the man made a move toward Adele. "The judge is off limits."

"Not to me, she isn't." Though the man was

shorter than Brian, he managed to look down his nose at him. "I'm Senator Ortega. Let me by."

Ah. Now Brian understood why the guy seemed familiar. The senator never missed an opportunity to be seen on camera. There was talk he planned to make a run for the presidency. Brian had no issue with the man's policies or political ambitions. But he wasn't getting anywhere near Adele. "Sorry, no can do. The judge is being assessed for injuries."

Ortega frowned. "You let me pass, young man, or I will have your badge."

No doubt the senator was used to getting his way. Brian stood his ground. "You can try."

"We'll see how easy it is." Senator Ortega turned away and brought out his phone. He spoke in hushed tones to whomever was on the other end of the call. Moments later, he turned, holding the phone out. "Your boss."

Acid bubbled into Brian's throat. The man had gone behind his back like some tattletale on the schoolyard. Brian snatched the phone from Ortega's hand and lifted it to his ear. "Boss?"

"Let him pass," Gavin said. "Apparently, he and the judge have a history. Besides, he's our state senator. He was in the building at the time of the explosions."

As if there weren't bad men in politics? Brian made a face. "I understand."

"I'm on my way to you now," Gavin said before hanging up.

Brian handed back the phone to Senator Ortega. Then he turned to Adele. "Judge Weston, Senator Ortega would like a word. Will you talk with him?"

"Of course, she will," the senator bellowed.

Brian kept his gaze on Adele. There was a flash of something in her eyes before her expression shuttered and she gave a slow nod. "Let him through."

Shoulders tense with distaste, Brian stepped aside to let the senator rush past him. Ortega sat beside Adele, putting his arm around her and pulling her in close. Brian couldn't prevent his fingers from curling into fists at his sides. He had no claim on Adele, yet the sight of another man being so familiar with her burned through his gut.

He spun away and gestured for a nearby patrolman to join him. Brian's gaze swept over the sea of media and other gawkers, looking for a threat, and attempting to ignore the cozy scene of the judge and the senator.

Apparently, there *was* history between the two. A strange sensation clawed its way through

Brian's chest. Jealousy? No way. He barely knew Adele. He had no feelings for her beyond those tied to him doing his job. Sure, he thought her attractive and interesting, but she'd made it clear she wasn't interested in him long ago. He didn't care who she saw in her private life. He just didn't like having his authority usurped. That was the cause of his internal fuming.

US marshal Gavin Armstrong joined Brian. "Sitrep."

Snapping to his attention to his boss, Brian gave a situation report, also known as a "sitrep."

"Judge hit her head. And has a gash on her leg. The security guard looked like a possible heart attack in progress. The court clerk is unconscious but stable."

Gavin gave a curt nod. "The courtroom had three devices. One under the judge's bench. And one attached beneath the prosecutor's table and the defendant's table," Gavin said. "Bomb technicians are searching the whole building for any more explosives."

Brian blew out a breath. "What does Tomas Garcia have to say?"

"I'm heading to the hospital to find out now," his boss said. "I hope he can shed some light on who wants him dead."

"I'll go with you." Brian would like a crack at questioning the man.

Gavin arched an eyebrow. "Her protection—" Gavin gestured with his chin toward Adele "—is your only mission for the foreseeable future."

Brian ground his back teeth. Protecting the one woman in Texas who wanted nothing to do with him was going to be torture.

Panic flared within Adele's chest. As if being bombed then having the hunky marshal carry her out of her chambers hadn't been enough to freak her out, the one person in the whole state she really would rather avoid had pushed his way to her side.

Sitting on the back bumper of the ambulance, she suffered through a quick hug from Senator John Ortega. When he left his arm encircling her shoulders, it took everything in her not to shake him off and jump to her feet.

It was odd really. They'd known each other for years. She'd met his then wife, now ex, on several occasions before she'd moved out of state after their divorce. John had always been kind toward her, even while making advances that she deflected. But he'd always kept to the boundaries she'd put up. Getting involved with the senator wasn't a good idea.

Not that she had plans to get involved with anyone. But she didn't want the public to question her judgeship or get the idea that she was in the pocket of any political party.

Today, John was crossing the line. And she didn't like it.

His touch sent frissons of unease sliding down her back.

Her gaze lifted and met Brian's. There was anger etched in his handsome face. No doubt he didn't appreciate the senator's high-handedness. Neither did she.

Unable to maintain the pretense of appreciating the senator's concern, she shifted to dislodge John's arm from around her shoulders. She didn't want him to touch her.

She'd had no compulsion to do the same with Brian when he'd held her close to his chest. In fact, she'd melted into his embrace. Feeling safe for the first time in longer than she could remember.

Too bad it was an illusion. She wasn't safe. Ever.

She couldn't let down her guard. Because when she did, something bad happened to anyone around her. She didn't know how she'd handle another tragedy. She sent up another silent plea to God for Rachel to heal from the explosion.

"Can you tell me what happened?" John asked. "The only information I've been given was that there was an explosion in your courtroom. It rocked the whole building. I was in a meeting."

Easing farther from him, Adele replied, "Yes, a bomb was planted beneath my bench." Though she remembered there being more explosions after the first one. "There had to have been secondary exploding devices in the courtroom."

The senator gasped. "More than one? Were you the target?"

"I don't know," she said, unable to keep the irritation from leaking into her tone. "I'm sure the marshals service and the local PD and the FBI and the CIA and the ATF, and every other agency of the alphabet soup, will dig into the explosion."

As if she needed to tell him this. She reined in her annoyance, realizing she was taking out her frustration and fright on this man who was trying to be kind. "I'm sorry. This has just been a lot."

"Of course, my dear," John said, waving away her apology, which sent a fresh wave of irritation through her. She didn't like being dismissed. "No need to apologize. Anyone would be on edge after surviving such an ordeal."

She glanced at him. "I don't know that I was

meant to survive." If she hadn't bumped into the device, she wouldn't have had cause to look beneath the bench and see it in time to get away.

John's expression remained passively concerned. "We will get to the bottom of this. I will keep you safe. Once the paramedics release you, I will take you home. I can arrange for your protection."

A fresh wave of panic crashed through her system. No way was she going to put her life into the senator's control. "I can manage to get home on my own. Thank you."

She could go home to her parents' house.

Not that she wanted to put her family in danger. But she certainly didn't want the attention of the senator. Her gaze zeroed in once again on Brian. His green eyes were narrowed on her as he and his boss stood talking a few feet away. His body was angled so that he could assess the crowd gathering while keeping an eye on her.

For some reason, his presence made her feel better. That also made her uncomfortable.

Time she took charge of the situation.

She stood. John also rose, a frown marring his handsome face.

"Thank you for your concern, Senator Ortega," she told him. "I'm sure you must be anxious to check on the prosecutor."

The two men were friends, from what she had gathered over the years.

"John." His voice was filled with mild censure. "And yes, of course, I will check on Prosecutor Fitch. But first, I will see you home."

Adele sent up a quick prayer that God would help her through this. It was like navigating shark-infested waters. The only boat providing safety was the tall US marshal stepping to her side. She didn't want to rely on Brian. Though, it didn't make any sense. It was his job to protect her. He was trained for the duty. But there was something about him that also called to her in ways she didn't understand or want.

"The marshals service will be providing protection for Judge Weston," Brian said, clearly having overheard John. "And I can guarantee you she will be well cared for. My boss will concur."

It was on the tip of Adele's tongue to tell both men to leave her alone. She didn't need either one of them. But, honestly, she did. She needed Brian, at least to get her away from the situation. If the cartel's aim had been to stop today's proceedings, they'd only managed a delay. Until the trial was over, she would need protection.

As much as it sent her nerves jingling and her senses reeling, she had to make the choice.

"Again, thank you, John. But Deputy Forrester will be overseeing my protection detail."

Whether he wanted to or not.

"If that is what you want," John said, shooting a glare at Brian.

Adele didn't want to pit the two men against each other. But this was her life. She'd promised herself a long time ago she would be the one in charge of her own destiny. She wasn't about to break the promise she'd made to herself. "It is."

She may or may not come to regret the decision she'd made to forgo Senator John Ortega's offer of help. Time would tell. She was loath to analyze the reason she'd chosen Brian over John. Maybe her decision stemmed from the surety that if she'd agreed to let John see her home, he would interpret the concession as an invitation to be more involved in her life. Not going to happen.

With Brian, there would be an expiration date on his attention. As soon as the courtroom bomber was caught, she'd be free to live her life.

"Now that that is settled…" Brian's voice was a tad too chipper for her liking. She narrowed her gaze on him as he continued. "Let's get you home."

"I want to check on my staff." Determined

to do just that, she stepped away only to have Brian snag her by the elbow, drawing her up against him.

"We can get a situation report on them later," he said, his intense gaze boring into her. "Your safety is paramount."

"That's what I've been saying. Maybe you can talk sense into her," John said with a clear plaintive tone.

After grinding her teeth at John's irritating words and extracting herself from Brian's touch, she managed to say politely to the senator, "Shouldn't you go check on Prosecutor Fitch?"

"Of course." John's expression softened. "Adele, if you need anything, you let me know. Promise me."

His concern was genuine. He really did care. Guilt pricked her conscience and she fought to stay true to her decision. Sentiment wouldn't derail her course now. "I will, John. Thank you."

Holding her gaze for a moment, his thoughts inscrutable, John nodded and then faced Brian, his expression hardening. "If anything happens to her, I will hold you accountable."

Brian inclined his head but the impatience in his eyes was unmistakable. "Duly noted."

Obviously, Brian didn't like being threatened. But who did? Adele watched the senator move away, his stride confident while he deftly talked to the press, certainly giving good sound bites for the news cycle. John did like to shine. Maybe that was what kept her from allowing him into her life. She didn't want the limelight.

Some would say being a judge disproved that idea, but from the bench she was an observer who kept a neutral stance. Her function was to guide and see that rules were followed.

The moment the senator was out of earshot, she said to Brian, "Thank you."

Mild surprise flared in Brian's green eyes. "For what?"

Not wanting to admit her relief at being out from beneath the senator's attentions, she said, "I would appreciate it if you investigated who blew up my courtroom and why."

His eyebrows dipped. "A full investigation will be done."

Adele refused to flinch beneath the intensity of his narrowed green-eyed gaze. Did he think to intimidate her? She'd faced down arrogant lawyers, malicious criminals, and everything in between. She'd developed a thick shell that not even a handsome US deputy marshal would be able to breach.

"I'm sticking close to you," he murmured so low she almost imagined the words.

Her mouth dried. He was declaring his intention. Sticking close to her. "What exactly does that mean?"

"Twenty-four-seven. Around-the-clock protection. Where you go, I go. Just consider me a part of your world from now on."

Her chest grew tight. This was of her own doing. She'd chosen the deputy over John. Now she had to squirm her way out of the decision she'd made. "It's really not necessary. I only told John you would be providing me protection to make him back off. Clearly, the bombing today was meant to take out Tomas Garcia. I'm confident I am no longer in danger. And your protection is not needed."

"As much as I appreciate your confidence that you are no longer in danger, I beg to differ." Brian widened his stance and crossed his arms over his broad chest.

The stubborn line of his jaw didn't bode well.

"We don't know who the intended target was or why," he continued. "Yes, it could have been an attempt on Garcia's life. But assumptions always leave a bad taste in my mouth. Until we have answers, you are mine to protect."

THREE

An antsy restlessness had Adele tapping her foot, which caused a riot of pain in her thigh. She clenched her jaw and froze. She was wasting time arguing with the man. Best to go along for now until she could extricate herself from the circumstances. "Fine. But I need to check on my staff before we leave. I will not be *settled* until I know that they are all right."

"If the paramedics are ready to release you, then we will check on your staff."

Adele wasn't sure what to make of his acquiescence but decided not to push him any further. She turned to the paramedic standing by, pretending not to listen. "Well? Can I leave?"

"Ma'am, I suggest you let us take you to the hospital for sutures. The butterfly bandages may not hold for long. And I'd recommend a head CT. You have a contusion on your forehead."

"I'm standing upright. I know my name. I'm good," Adele countered.

"I'll make sure she is seen by a doctor," Brian interjected.

The paramedic nodded and handed Adele a clipboard. "Please sign here that you are declining transport."

Quickly signing the document, she handed back the clipboard. "I appreciate your concern and your help today. I'm sure there are others who could use your assistance."

Once the paramedic walked away, she said to Brian, "Now, may I see to my staff?"

"As you wish." He gestured for her to precede him.

She frowned, wondering if he'd quoted from her favorite movie on purpose?

But she was not some farm girl to his farm boy.

There would be no happily-ever-after, riding off on a white horse.

She strode away from the ambulance, aware of Brian right on her heels. With each step, her leg throbbed. Soon, she couldn't keep from limping. She started when Brian stepped closer and put an arm around her waist, taking some of her weight.

"Lean on me," he said.

That was the last thing she wanted to do. She didn't want to need anyone. Doing so would only end badly. But in this instance, she had to take his offered help. Her objective was the well-being of her staff, and the price was having to rely on Deputy Brian Forrester.

Aware of the many gazes tracking them as she allowed Brian to help her, they walked around to the front of the building where the police officers had set up a barricade to keep the media at bay.

"What's up with you and the senator?" Brian asked.

The heat from his touch burned through her judge's robe. "Nothing."

"Didn't seem like nothing," he murmured.

She didn't respond. No way would she confide that the senator wanted more than a friendship from her or the reasons she'd chosen to avoid romantic entanglements. The past needed to stay in the past. Yet the significance of the parole hearing notice in her pocket weighed heavy on her and raised so many questions. Questions that she couldn't pursue the answers for at the moment.

As they approached his boss, Adele straightened away from Brian but was careful to keep weight off her injured leg. She searched the area, but all she saw was the swarm of jurors and more courthouse employees among the emergency personnel and media.

"Marshal Armstrong," Adele said, "can you please tell me what has happened to my staff?"

"Judge Weston," Marshal Armstrong said, "your injured staff members have been transported to the hospital for care."

Adele swallowed the panic and fear and sorrow clogging her throat. Though they were staff and she couldn't claim a close relationship with any of them, she still felt the weight of responsibility for their welfare. "I heard that Rachel Brown was in critical condition. Is she alive?"

"Last I heard, yes," Gavin replied.

Somewhat relieved to hear this, Adele turned to Brian. "I'll go to the hospital now."

The marshal and Brian exchanged a look rife with lots of meaning that Adele wasn't quite sure how to interpret. But she didn't care. She wouldn't be put off. "Now, please."

Gavin's gaze probed her before he said, "Deputy Forrester will take you to the hospital then he'll take you home."

Brian nodded to his boss. "Can I have the keys to one of the vehicles?"

Marshal Armstrong tugged keys from his

pocket. "Take my rig. Jace and I will take his to the hospital."

Accepting the keys, Brian said, "Yes, sir."

Another marshal jogged up to them. A tall man with brown hair and hooded eyes beneath a cowboy hat. He gave her an assessing once-over before his gaze flicked to Brian. "This must be the judge."

"Judge Weston," Gavin said, "this is Deputy Jace Armstrong."

Surprise washed over her. "Your son?"

Jace grinned, transforming his demeanor. He was a handsome man, but he didn't make her heart flutter the way Brian did. Though why she was even making a comparison between the two marshals, she didn't know. She gave herself a mental head slap. Her judgment when it came to men was faulty. Best to ignore any inclining of attraction or emotional attachment. Brian was only a means to an end and wouldn't be around too long.

"I am the marshal's son," Jace said. "Though sometimes he doesn't like to admit it."

Marshal Armstrong rolled his eyes. "Not true." He shifted his focus to Brian. "We'll see you at the hospital." To his son, he said, "Let's go talk to Tomas Garcia. You're driving."

The two men walked away. Adele looked up

at Brian, saw the small frown marring his expression. "Do you regret not being able to go with them?"

He faced her, his countenance transforming into a vestige of charm, sending her heart rate soaring. "What?" He cocked his head as if puzzled, but there was amusement in his eyes. "And give up the prettiest assignment I've had in a very long time?"

Adele dipped her chin. No, no, no. She didn't want this man charming her even though his grin made her stomach do little flip-flops and his words seeped into the edges of her defenses.

Steeling herself against his appeal, she said, "Can we please go now?"

"Right this way. Your chariot awaits." He tightened his hold around her and guided her toward the black unmarked SUV waiting near the curb.

The moment she settled into the SUV and buckled her seat belt, Adele slumped down and rested against the doorframe as if the exhaustion of living through a bombing had finally caught up to her. And she was hurting, if the grimace twisting her pretty face was any indication.

Brian really needed to get her to the hospital where she could get some pain relief. Though he doubted she would take anything. She seemed the type who would grit it out. He couldn't fault her because he was the same.

A disturbing prickle at the back of Brian's neck had his muscles tensing and his nerves stretching taut as he drove through the chaotic downtown San Antonio traffic. He kept one eye on the rearview mirror. A white sedan had pulled out onto the road after them when they'd left the courthouse parking lot and was staying at least four cars behind as they crossed town.

Instead of going left toward the hospital, he took a sudden right, heading back downtown.

Adele grabbed the dashboard. "What are you doing? The hospital's that way."

Deciding not to sugarcoat the situation or keep anything from her, he said, "We have a tail."

"Are you sure?" She twisted in her seat to stare through the back window. "There's a lot of traffic. How can you know that any of the cars are intentionally following us?"

Slanting her a glance, he couldn't keep the dryness from his tone, "I've been at this job for a long time. I can spot a tail."

She swiveled to stare at him. "I'm not questioning your abilities."

He flashed her a grin. "Good to know."

"It's most likely the media," she said. "Is my going to the hospital a secret?"

"Not a secret." But getting her home undetected would be a priority. At the next stoplight, he slowed despite the green light. When the light turned red, instead of stopping, he hit the gas and sped through the intersection, hooked a left, crossing traffic and leaving behind a blare of screeching tires and honking horns.

He could feel Adele's startled gaze on him.

Slowly, she peeled her fingers off the vinyl dashboard. "If I didn't have a headache before, I certainly do now. Thanks."

He grimaced, not liking that he'd added to her pain or the barely detected quiver in her tone. But he had to admire this woman's spunk. No hysterics. No barrage of "poor me."

Pulling into the four-story parking garage, he took the ramp to the third floor where he knew they could step right into the hospital without having to take an elevator or the stairs. Choosing a spot near the entrance, he backed into the space. He preferred wheels facing front for a quicker exit.

When Adele reached for the door handle, he put out a hand, stopping short of touching her. "Sit tight. I'll come around."

"I'm perfectly—"

"No."

She heaved a sigh but put her hand back in her lap. He popped open his door and stepped out, shutting the door behind him then locking the doors. He stood, listening, waiting for anything to trip his internal warning system that had saved his life in the past, leaving him with only a few scars.

After a heartbeat, he walked around to the passenger's-side door, again pausing for one second longer. He took a breath. Though he believed he'd lost their tail, the need for caution demanded he be alert.

If it were up to him, he'd take her far out of town to a rural hospital where there would be little chance of anyone bothering her. But she wouldn't go easily or quietly. She wanted to personally check on her staff. And his boss was expecting him here. He hit the fob, unlocking the doors.

Before he could even reach for the handle, she popped the door open and pushed it into him. "I do not like being locked in."

She hopped out, ignoring his extended hand, and winced as her injured leg hit the ground. Stubborn woman.

He shoved the door shut and armed the vehicle's alarm. He put his hand to her back.

She stiffened and stepped away. "Do you know where my staff are?"

Checking his phone as they walked inside, he noted Jace had texted that were already on site at the hospital. Brian shot off a quick text letting Jace know they were on their way inside. "Twelfth floor."

They took the elevator. Passing the nurses' station, he nodded to the curious hospital staff and kept Adele moving toward the cluster of US marshals at the end of the hall. Gavin and Jace stepped away from the other marshals.

"The judge needs to be seen," Brian told his boss.

Adele shot him a glare. "After I check my staff."

"Judge Weston," Gavin said, his gaze bouncing between Adele and Brian, "I agree with my deputy. Let's have your injuries seen by a doctor. Then we will direct you to your staff."

"The paramedics did a fine job assessing me. They released me." Adele's firm tone suggested she was ready for a fight.

"Only at your insistence," Brian interjected, hoping to head her off. "The paramedic recommended you be seen by a doctor. That is what's going to happen."

Without waiting for her permission, he waved to one of the gawking nurses. "We need a doctor to examine her wounds."

"Right away," the young nurse said and hurried off. Presumably to get a doctor.

Another nurse stepped up. "Let's get you in a room. This way."

Adele glared at him then heaved a sigh and lifted her chin as she followed the nurse to an exam room.

Brian moved to follow them when Gavin said, "Brian, I want you to join us while we question Tomas."

"But the judge—" Despite not wanting this assignment, he took his duties seriously.

"She will be perfectly safe." Gavin gestured for another deputy marshal to join them. "Conlan, you stay here. Don't let anybody in."

Deputy Joe Conlan, late twenties, tall, with close-cropped hair beneath a brown cowboy hat, took a position by the door. "Yes, sir."

Brian didn't know Conlan very well. The younger man had come on after Brian had transferred to the California office. Sometime in the year or so he'd been gone, there were a few new deputies on board and a few who'd transferred to other offices. Like Jace. Brian often wondered if finding love and changing his whole life for a woman would turn out well for his friend. He prayed so, even if Brian knew he would never succumb to that fate.

Sparing one last glance at the closed door, he moved down the hall with his boss and Jace. Two US deputy marshals, who were part of the prison transport system, stood outside an exam room. Both of the men nodded as Gavin led the way into the room.

Tomas Garcia lay propped up in the hospital bed, both hands cuffed to the railings on either side of him, his legs shackled to the footboard. Monitors beeped. An IV dripped into his arm. The man looked ages older than he had the last time Brian had laid eyes on him. His cheeks had sunken. His once-thick hair had thinned. His dark eyes, however, had lost none of their menace.

"To what do I owe this torture?" Tomas asked.

"We have some questions," Gavin said.

Tomas turned his face away. "I don't have answers."

"It would be in your best interest if you did," Jace said.

That gained Tomas's attention. "How's that?"

"Who tried to kill you today?" Brian asked.

Tomas narrowed his gaze. "Why do you think it was an assassination attempt on me?"

"One of the explosive devices was under the table you were sitting at," Jace said.

Eyes widening with shock, Tomas clenched his jaw.

Gavin moved to the bedside. "If the judge hadn't noticed the bomb under her bench, you would be dead right now."

"And so would she," Tomas shot back.

Brian fisted his hands. "Did you do this? Was this an attempt to kill the judge?"

"Why would I want to kill myself?" Tomas's brow furrowed. "That makes no sense."

"Then who wants you dead?" Brian asked once again. They needed to find the culprit and verify that the judge wasn't the target.

Tomas shrugged. "Any number of people."

"We can't protect you if we don't know who has it out for you," Jace said.

"Why would you want to protect me?" Tomas's voice held contempt. "I thought my demise would make you marshals happy."

"As much as we want you out of business, we're not in the business of killing people," Gavin assured him.

Tomas's eyes hardened and zeroed on Jace. "Tell that to Marco."

"What happened to your son was self-defense," Jace said, his tone harsh. "And you know it."

Tomas's lips twisted. "So you say. Why should I believe you?"

Jace shook his head. "You're unbelievable. You've seen the bank's video footage. You know your son tried to kidnap Abby Frost with the intent to kill her in some weird revenge scheme because she and I escaped your compound and testified before a grand jury to what you and Marco did to us."

Abby and Jace had been forced to flee Washington State when Tomas had sent men to kidnap Abby in the hopes of drawing out her biological father, who had witnessed Marco commit murder.

"I know no such thing," Tomas replied, his dark eyes flashing with anger and grief.

Needing to keep the situation from spiraling beyond the issue at hand, Brian said, "Someone has taken control of your cartel. Or what's left of it." He watched closely for Garcia's reaction.

The older man made a dismissive noise and would have waved off the notion if his hands weren't handcuffed to the bed. "No way would my people allow a rival cartel to take over. You're wrong."

"Who's calling the shots then?" Gavin pressed.

Brian could see Tomas's mind working.

"Maybe we should just put you in general lockup until the trial starts," Jace said. "If you're so unconcerned by the threat against you."

Panic flared in Tomas's eye. "You wouldn't dare. I wouldn't last a day in general."

"Then help us help you," Gavin said.

"I'll give you a name, if you move me to Alderson federal facility."

Brian scoffed. "No way." Tomas wasn't a celebrity with money and power. He was nothing more than a thug.

"I'll talk to the attorney general, and we'll see what we can do, but only if you give me a name," Gavin said.

Surprised his boss was willing to make any concessions to the man who'd nearly killed his son, Brian stared at Gavin. Really?

Tomas sighed, seemingly weighing his options. Then, finally, he said, "Maria Montoya."

Brian exchanged questioning glances with both Jace and Gavin. Maybe Sera would have come across the name in her research on Garcia's cartel.

"We need a little more than that," Gavin said. "Who is she? And why is she trying to kill you?"

"If what you say is true, that somebody is trying to take over my organization, then it would be her. She's the only one who has any legitimate claim." Tomas winced. "Rather, illegitimate claim."

Brian played the word *illegitimate* through his brain. "Your daughter?"

Garcia's gaze snapped to Brian. "Give the marshal a gold star."

"Where do we find this Maria Montoya?" Gavin asked.

Shrugging, Tomas said, "How should I know? I haven't seen her since she was an infant."

The man was despicable. Brian had no patience for anyone who shirked their responsibilities. His own parents fell into that category. Divorced multiple times and never really too interested in the son they'd produced.

"I want a guarantee," Tomas insisted.

"I'll talk to the AG. That's as good as it gets." Gavin turned on his heel and walked out the door. Jace and Brian followed.

"Do we believe him?" Jace asked. "Nothing in our investigation brought up that he had an illegitimate daughter hidden away somewhere."

"Get Seraphina on it," Gavin said. "Brian, stay close to the judge until we verify that this truly was a hit on Tomas Garcia."

"You got it, sir." He had no plans to leave her side. He relieved Conlan at the door to the judge's exam room.

A few moments later, the door opened and the doctor walked out.

"How is she?" Brian asked.

"You'll have your hands full with that one," the doctor told him with a smile. "We stitched up her wound. She'll be fine once the swelling goes down. No signs of concussion. She's good to go."

"Understatement," Adele said as she stepped out of the room still wearing her black judge's robe. "Can you tell me where I can find my staff?"

"The nurse will give you directions." The doctor walked away.

The nurse informed them that Rachel Brown, the court reporter, was in surgery. Brian elicited a promise from the nurse to call with an update. After visiting for a few minutes with the court bailiff and then her judicial assistant, Brian insisted it was time to leave.

"You're exhausted and it's starting to show," he told Adele.

"Thanks," she said without much heat, which only confirmed to Brian the woman was losing steam fast.

They took the elevator to the third floor and stepped through the sliding-glass doors into the parking garage.

A white sedan sat idling halfway down the parking aisle. Shadows darkened the front windshield, obscuring the driver. Wariness set off alarms in Brian's system.

Tucking Adele into his side, Brian placed his hand on his weapon. "Back inside, now."

The driver's-side window lowered, a black muzzle appeared, and the driver fired. The loud retort echoed off the stone walls. Bits of concrete spit up at their legs. Adele gasped. Heart jolting, Brian shoved her toward the safety of the glass doors and was gratified she didn't hesitate to run.

Pulling his weapon free, he returned fire, hitting the sedan and shattering the front windshield. The car reversed, spun 180 degrees, swiping the end of a luxury coupe, and shot forward, disappearing as it sped out of the parking garage with an ear-piercing squeal of tires.

Replacing his weapon in its holster, Brian grabbed his phone, called Dispatch and reported the attack, giving the dispatcher the make and model of the sedan as well as the first three letters of the license plate.

"Brian?"

He turned to find Adele standing in the hospital doorway. Her topaz eyes were wide with shock.

Moving swiftly to her side, he ushered her farther into the hospital. She trembled beneath his hand.

"What was that?" she asked.

"Someone tried to kill you. Again."

FOUR

The roar of blood rushing through her veins prevented Adele from registering Brian's words. His hand at her elbow firmly propelled her further away from the hospital parking garage where, just moments before, someone had shot at them.

If Brian hadn't shoved her toward the hospital entrance, she could have been killed.

He could have been killed.

His words finally made sense.

Someone tried to kill you. Again.

Emotions clogged her throat. Her chest tightened, squeezing her lungs and restricting her breathing. She gulped for air and reached for the wall, needing something to support her, to keep her upright. Brian's hand on her elbow tightened, an anchor in a storm.

Someone tried to kill her.

Again.

She lifted her gaze to meet Brian's. "You believe the bombing at the courthouse was meant for me?"

He didn't answer, but the grim set of his mouth and the hard glint in his eyes confirmed what he didn't verbalize. Someone wanted her dead. Why? Who?

The realization hit her like a wrecking ball. Until this moment, she hadn't really accepted that her life was in danger.

In a rush, the air trapped in her lungs swooshed out. The world went sideways. No, she was tilting.

Brian gripped her biceps. "Stay with me. You can do this. Breathe."

The sounds of thumping feet penetrated beyond the pulse pounding in her ears and sent a fresh ribbon of fear winding its way through her and tying her up in knots. Brian pressed her back against the wall, pivoted and used his body as a shield. He reached for his weapon. Her lungs seized. Nausea roiled in her stomach.

Two marshals, Jace and Gavin Armstrong, rushed out of the stairwell. The elevator dinged and the doors slid open, revealing three hospital security guards. The men eased out with weapons drawn.

"Whoa, it's okay," Jace said to the security

guards. "US marshals." Jace skidded to a halt in front of Brian. "Dude, we heard gunshots."

Brian's shoulders relaxed and he holstered his weapon.

Despite the apparent lack of immediate danger, Adele couldn't take in air. A buzzing inside her head had her muscles tightening.

The men crowded around them. Their questions came fast and furious.

"Did you see the shooter?"

"Are you hurt?"

"Where did they go?"

The urge to flee was a palpable thing, but there was nowhere for her to run with her back against the wall. The rumble of Brian's voice moored her in place.

Police sirens echoed off the concrete parking garage and assaulted her ears. Her head pounded. Moments later, San Antonio police officers flooded into the entryway with additional questions.

The cacophony of voices battered her, conjuring up images from the past. There had been so much blood. The campus security guard dead at her feet. Police officers pressing in, bombarding her with questions. She hadn't been able to speak. Her throat had closed from the horror of what she'd been through, preventing her from explaining. She'd hyperventilated and had to be sedated. The terrifying scenes played like a flipbook through her brain, going faster and faster.

"Adele. Adele."

Brian's insistent voice reverberated through her, drawing her back to the present horror of being shot at and almost being blown into debris on the courthouse lawn. She still couldn't breathe. She clutched at her throat.

Brian's concerned face swam before her eyes. Sweat broke out on her back. A tremor worked its way through her. She was going to be sick.

She pushed at Brian, forcing him to step back, allowing her space, but it wasn't enough. It would never be enough.

Slipping past Brian, she bumped into the closest security guard like a pinball off a guardrail. She regained her footing and tore down the hospital hallway, needing to find a safe space, chased by the knowledge she was about to unravel. All the familiar signals sparking in her body tormented her.

She tried the handle of a door. Locked. She kept moving, desperation clouding her vision. From behind, she could hear Brian calling her name, but she couldn't respond. Didn't dare stop. She needed to be alone. His thunderous footsteps as he charged down the hall after her drove her to move more quickly. The next doorknob turned in her hand and she flung the door open. An empty supply room.

She rushed inside, but before she could close the door and turn the lock, Brian was there, filling the doorway. Light from the hallway made him appear menacing, intimidating, before he closed the door behind him. Irrational fear filled her. A scream built inside her chest. She clamped a hand over her mouth and shrank further into the supply room.

The overhead light came on with her motion. She backed into a supply rack, knocking toilet paper and tissue boxes off the shelves to rain down on her head. She sank to the ground to sit among the scattered paper products, pulling her knees to her chest and curling forward like a pill bug.

Please, oh, God. Please, oh God. Please, oh God. The plea whispered through her brain, through her being, and she shuddered. Her heart hammered against her rib cage. Another wave of nausea washed over her as the sickening realization smacked into her. She gagged.

She'd almost cost Brian his life. Another hero would have been lost because of her.

Big, strong hands gently stroked down her

arms, smoothed her hair from her face. A callused hand lifted her chin. She squeezed her eyes closed, not wanting to reveal her inner torment.

"Adele, you're safe. I'm not going to let anything happen to you."

Brian's soft, soothing tone was meant to comfort.

A sob escaped her.

He didn't understand. This wasn't about her. He had protected her, but he could have died.

A fingertip traced the outer edge of her ear as he pushed a lock of hair back. "Adele, I need you to hold it together. We'll get through this. Trust me. But I need you to be strong."

She'd heard those words before. Her father telling her to be strong. Her lawyer telling her to be strong. Her mother and her friends all wanting—no, needing—her to be strong.

In the dark days after the attack in college, when she had finally found her voice, the mantra *You have to be strong* had been a lifeline. Only, the damage had been done. A man had died, and she'd been left with the horror of memories and panic.

But now she could do something to prevent a future tragedy.

She opened her eyes and stared hard at this attractive, caring man who had saved her life.

Rationally, she knew he was trained to put himself in the line of fire. He was a man of action, a man who ran toward danger instead of away. Having someone protect her was a necessity. Hadn't she grown accustomed to seeing the bailiff in her courtroom every day?

As a prosecutor and now a judge, she'd become familiar with the animosity directed at her, but the difference this time was that someone was actively trying to harm her with no regard for collateral damage. But who? Why? And what if Brian paid the ultimate price?

Pushing his hand away, she scrambled to her feet. "You have to go. I can't do this with you. You could have died. I can't—I can't—" Her words faltered, lodged in her throat. The rising panic once again threatened to unravel her.

Brian's arms snaked around her, pulling her to his chest. Shock had her stiffening. Her hands lay trapped at her sides. She arched back, trying to break his lock on her. But he held her firmly, gently.

"No one died." His soft voice threaded through her like silk.

It was only by the grace of God they all had survived the explosion, but Rachel was still in critical condition. All because someone wanted her dead.

"I know this was traumatic for you," he continued, his voice wrapping around her, cozy and comforting. "But you're safe. I'm safe. Please, trust me."

Despite his assurances, she shuddered and tilted her head to stare up at him. "But you could have died. Don't you get it? I can't let something happen to you."

A lopsided grin spread across his face. Her knees threatened to give out. How could she find him attractive at a time like this?

"Darlin', you don't have to worry about me. My job is to keep *you* safe. You're the priority."

Frustration swamped her and she groaned. She shook her head, a protest rising. But before she could put voice to the words to convince him he was wrong, the door to the supply closet opened. She shrank back.

Marshal Gavin Armstrong stuck his head inside. "Are we good in here?"

"The judge is suffering from shock," Brian replied. "A nurse?"

"You got it." Gavin disappeared, shutting the door behind him.

"I don't need a nurse," Adele grumbled, though even to her own ears there wasn't much heat in her words.

"Of course not. But humor me, please." Brian soothed a hand down her back.

The rhythmic motion calmed her nerves. Her limbs turned languid. The comfort and security he offered was more than she could resist. She melted into his arms, her cheek resting against his chest. Somewhere in the back of her mind, she realized he had on a Kevlar vest beneath his shirt. The knowledge wiped away the last of her panic.

Her arms slipped around his waist and she clung to him. But soon she'd have to let go. She couldn't cling to him outside of the closet. She had to figure out a way to survive her fear alone. Something she'd struggled to accomplish for longer than she'd care to admit.

Brian's heart twisted in his chest. Adele was worried about him. Her panic stemmed from a fear he'd die because of her. Not one utterance of concern for her own safety. How rare. And totally touching.

He tightened his hold on her. It was his job to protect this beautiful and kind woman. He would do everything in his power to keep her safe. There was no doubt in his mind that she was in danger. Someone had tried to kill her twice. Though the bombing at the courthouse had been made to look as if the whole proceedings had been in jeopardy, having the driver of the sedan shoot at Adele made it very clear she had been the intended target to begin with.

If this was some kind of trick by Tomas Garcia, what did he hope to gain by eliminating the judge? A new judge would be assigned to his case. Did he just intend to kill every judge in the state? That was senseless. But then, Brian wasn't sure how stable Garcia was. Some mysterious daughter trying to kill him? Did he really expect them to buy the outlandish tale?

But if Garcia wasn't trying to hurt the judge, then the threat to Adele's life must be tied to one of her other cases. Or something from her past?

Either way, she needed him to keep her safe. And he would do whatever it took to protect her.

The door to the supply closet opened and the nurse they'd talked with earlier stepped in, carrying a small disposable cup and a bottled water. "The doctor prescribed this antianxiety medication for Judge Weston."

Adele shook her head. "No drugs."

Brian leaned back so he could stare into her lovely, tear-stained face. "The medication will help you. It won't knock you out." He looked to the nurse for confirmation.

"Exactly," the brunette said. "This will take the edge off. These won't harm you in any way. I promise."

Brian held Adele's gaze. "Do it for me."

She released her hold on him and turned to the nurse. "What are they?"

The nurse rattled off the medication's name.

A parade of emotions played across the landscape of Adele's beautiful face. She closed her eyes for a heartbeat. When she regained her composure, resolve shone in her features. "A half of one."

The nurse gave a nod. Brian decided it was better than nothing. He needed Adele to be composed when they left here. As soon as word got out that there had been a shooting involving a judge, the press would show up wanting information. Information they didn't have. And he and Adele still needed to give their statements to San Antonio PD.

The nurse broke one of the tabs in two and dropped it into Adele's palm, then handed over the bottled water.

Adele took the medication and looked up at Brian. "It'll take about thirty minutes for it to really come into effect. Between now and then,

I need to get out of here. Because when it does take effect, I want to be home."

Surprise washed through Brian. Clearly, she had some experience with antianxiety medications. Had she had panic attacks like this before? Or was this a one-time situational episode? He wasn't about to question her now. Whatever got her to the safety of her house, he'd accept. "Understood."

Keeping her tucked into his side with an arm around her, they followed the nurse out of the supply room.

"Any news on Rachel Brown?" Adele asked the nurse.

"She successfully came through surgery. She had a ruptured spleen. Her prognosis is good." The nurse looked at Brian and gave him a smile. "I have your number. I'll call you if anything changes."

Brian returned the smile. "I'd appreciate it."

The nurse gave him a long lingering look before walking away. Beside him, he heard Adele give a little huff, drawing his attention, but she glanced away. With a hand to the small of Adele's back, he escorted her to the exit. A forensic team was already busy collecting bullet casings and photographing tire marks.

"We need to give our statements," Brian told Adele.

She nodded. "I understand."

He kept an eye on Adele as she talked with a female officer, while he spoke to another officer.

"We have the whole incident on video," Jace told them. "Hospital security alerted us, which is how we got down here so quickly."

"Is the shooter visible on the video?" Brian asked, hoping they could resolve this situation quickly.

"Unfortunately, no. The car windows were too tinted and the angle of the camera not conducive to a clear photo," Jace told him.

Brian let out a low growl of frustration. "I'll take the judge home now."

"I'll follow," Jace offered.

Brian was thankful for the backup. Getting the judge home safely was paramount. All of his questions as to why the judge was in danger and from whom would have to wait.

With Jace watching their six, they exited the hospital for a second time and made it to his boss's SUV without incident. Brian opened the passenger door and offered her his hand. There was the barest of hesitations before she slipped her hand over his, their palms pressed together as she climbed into the passenger seat.

He jogged around to the driver's side and hopped in. He plugged her address into the navigation system of the vehicle. The drive to the posh neighborhood outside the city limits was quiet save for the low volume of jazz music playing from the radio. Brian didn't dare touch the dial because his boss, Gavin, was very particular.

At the community entrance, Adele gave him the code to open the large iron gate. Jace honked and peeled away as Brian drove through the gate. He turned the vehicle down a cul-de-sac drive and parked in the driveway of the smallest house in the neighborhood, which was still massively impressive.

"Your house keys?" He held out his hand. "I'll make sure it's safe before you enter."

She frowned but dug through her purse and handed him a set of keys. "Highly unlikely anyone would be able to discover where I live. The deed is not under my name. It's under my father's corporation. And no one can get through the gate without a code."

"No security is infallible," he told her.

"The alarm code is four-five-four-six."

He stepped out of the SUV and went into

her house, making quick work of clearing each room. He didn't linger long enough to take in all the details, but he had the impression of a very modern, tidy home.

Helping Adele out of the SUV, he told her, "We're good. I noticed you have a dog kennel, but no dog."

"Scout is with the dog sitter. She'll drop him off soon."

At the front door, Adele paused and blocked the entrance. "You've seen me home. You can go now."

He cocked his head. Did she really believe she was sending him away? "What part of me sticking close to you did you forget about?"

Her gaze narrowed. "You can be unstuck to me now."

"No, ma'am," he said. "Until we have neutralized the threat against you, I'm here as your shadow for the duration."

She made a face and marched inside.

Suppressing a smile, Brian locked the door behind him and followed her into the kitchen. He leaned against the gleaming marble counter. She grabbed two bottles of water from the fridge. When she handed one to him, he gratefully took it. "Thank you. I promise you, Adele, you'll hardly even know I'm here."

She took a long swig from the water bottle. After briskly replacing the lid, she gave him a look rife with skepticism. "I doubt that very much." She headed down the hall but stopped when he made to follow. "I'm going to my bedroom. The one place you will not venture."

He saluted. "No problem, ma'am."

She rolled her eyes and disappeared behind the last door on the right.

Brian sank onto the French country blue leather couch and swept a hand down his face. He'd meant to discuss the panic attack with Adele before she'd disappeared into her room, but now he'd have to wait. He'd like to know if the episode at the hospital had been triggered purely by the high-stress situation or if panic attacks were something she dealt with on a regular basis.

For now, he'd be patient and take advantage of the downtime to decompress and formulate a plan to keep her safe. On two sides of Adele's house were her neighbors. But the backside of Adele's fenced yard butted up against the green expanse of the golf course. An easy access point. He made calls to the golf course management company to ascertain their level of security as well as calls to check on the neighbors. There was no such thing as overly cautious.

Two hours later, there was a noise at the front door. Brian vaulted to his feet and rushed to the window to look outside. Any view he might have had of the front door was obscured by the porch enclosure. With his hand on his weapon, he reached for the doorknob just as Adele rushed out from her bedroom.

"Deputy Forrester. Move away from the door."

He paused and turned to stare at her. Her auburn hair was loose about her shoulders, framing her delicate face. She'd changed into comfortable-looking lounge pants and a pink fuzzy sweater. Her feet were bare, revealing pink nail polish on her toes. His mouth went dry.

With effort, he pulled himself together with a frown. "Somebody's trying to get in."

She made an impatient gesture with her hand. "It's Teresa Watts, my dog sitter, and Scout."

He couldn't keep the skepticism from his tone. "How do you know?"

Adele tapped a finger on the smartwatch encircling her wrist. "I can see them on my screen." She stepped closer to him, put her hand on his chest and applied a bit of pressure. He backed up a few steps. "You'll only scare them."

"I thought you said I was charming." He couldn't refrain from teasing.

She wrinkled her nose at him, and he barked out a laugh.

"Scout's skittish around new people," she explained. "Especially men. He's a rescue and I think a man must have abused him as a pup."

Skittish like his owner. The last thing he needed was a dog charging him. Brian retreated a couple more steps but not so far away he couldn't reach out and grab Adele if needed. Regardless of how safe she believed her home to be, until they caught whomever was after her, he couldn't let his guard down.

FIVE

Adele suppressed amusement while watching her forty-five-pound Dalmatian sniff Brian. Scout's big old paws were on Brian's chest, and his snout stretched out to meet Brian's nose. Brian held himself still as if afraid her boy would attack.

Adele refrained from intervening. It was best to just let Scout discover for himself that Brian was a decent guy. She'd never seen Scout be overly aggressive. Nor had she seen him be so curious with a male guest, except with her dad.

She'd chalked up Scout's acceptance of her father as good judgment on the dog's part. Her dad was the best man she knew.

Was Scout's curiosity about Brian an indication the dog judged Brian to be an upright guy?

She had to admit, as far as she could tell, Brian was better than most.

He hadn't embarrassed her by sharing her

anxiety attack in the hospital with his colleagues. Though he had asked the nurse for meds. But that was expected. See a problem, throw medication at it.

She could only guess it must've been scary for him to see her so freaked out.

You have to be strong.

The words played on repeat through her head like a vinyl record with a scratch. She straightened her spine and squared her shoulders. She would be strong.

This maniac trying to kill her would not win.

The anxiety would not win.

She made a noise into her cheek. Scout's head snapped around, his eyes meeting hers. She gestured with her hand, palm face-out. The dog dropped away from Brian's chest and hurried to her side, putting his nose into her hand. She gave him a good scratch behind the ears and cooed that he was a good boy.

Then Scout leaned into her legs, his sign that he wanted more attention. Right now, she had other things to deal with. She turned to the dog sitter, who stared at Brian with rapt curiosity. Adele cleared her throat, drawing Teresa's focus. "I really appreciate you taking care of him. I don't think I'll need you tomorrow."

Adele sought Brian's gaze. He gave a nod.

Just as she suspected. There was no way she was going back to work tomorrow. Besides, her courtroom and judge's chamber would take days, if not weeks, to be put back in order. But the justice system would not sleep. She didn't know how much damage had been done to the courthouse as a whole. She assumed other cases would be heard in courtrooms that hadn't been damaged. She made a mental note to check.

A little *V* appeared between Teresa's dark blond brows. Her gaze bounced between Adele and Brian. "Okay, if you're sure."

"You were out with the dog all day?" Brian asked.

Confusion clouded Teresa's eyes. "I was. Is there a problem?"

"I'd like you to write out your itinerary for the day." Brian added, "And for the last few days."

Adele's mouth opened with a protest but a quelling look from Brian had her snapping her jaw shut. He didn't really consider Teresa capable of bombing the courthouse, didn't he?

"Sure, I can do that." Teresa shrugged. "I just need paper and pen."

With a sigh of resignation, Adele went to her entryway table, opened the middle drawer and pulled out a notepad and pencil. She handed both to Teresa. "You can sit at the dining table. He's a friend, and he's being overly cautious. There was some trouble at the courthouse this morning." No doubt, Teresa would see it in the news or read about it on the internet. "Nothing for you to worry about."

While Teresa sat and started writing, Adele pushed Brian out onto the patio then shut the sliding-glass door behind her and Scout. While the dog sniffed around the grass, she pointed a finger at Brian. "You can't honestly believe she had anything to do with what happened today?"

His direct look pierced through her. "Ma'am, I will leave no stone unturned in my duties to protect you."

"Don't 'ma'am' me," Adele said, irritated by how his use of the honorarium made her feel old. They had to be close to the same age. "Teresa is not a stone to be turned. She is my trusted dog sitter. Do you honestly think I didn't vet her before I hired her?"

Brian held up his hands. "Look, my job is to protect you. I can't do that if I don't know who we're dealing with and why they want to harm you. Everyone is suspect until they aren't."

She wanted to know who and why, as well. Earlier, she'd thought all she wanted was her normal life back, but how could anything be normal with this man underfoot in her home, crowding her space and digging into her life. "But wouldn't it be better for me if you were out there investigating?"

His lopsided grin appeared again. So appealing, it was hard to tear her eyes away from him to watch Scout chase a bee around the grass.

"I thought we'd already had this discussion," Brian said. "I'm here for the duration. Not going anywhere. I can investigate and protect you at the same time."

It took all her willpower not to retreat inside and lock him out. But she doubted even the triple locking mechanism she had on her sliding-glass door would prevent the determined US marshal from doing his job. He'd probably just lounge on the patio until he had a locksmith come out and remove the door lock.

Getting back to normal was going to look a little different for a while. But she was determined not to let this pushy, gorgeous marshal rattle her any more than he already had. She would have to trust that God would see her through this. Her faith in Jesus had never let her down. Sometimes her faith was the only way she managed to get through the day.

She patted her thigh to call Scout back to her. The dog trotted over and nudged her hand, but she didn't have a treat, so he wandered away. She sighed. "Fine. I will set you up in the guest-room once Teresa leaves. She doesn't need to know you're staying."

He rubbed a hand over his jaw, drawing her attention to the movement. "Hmm. Might be to our benefit if she does know I'm staying, in case she's an accomplice."

Adele jerked her gaze to his eyes and ground her back teeth. "Teresa is not an accomplice. Scout loves her."

Scout leaned against Brian's legs, begging for his attention. Apparently, the dog also thought Brian was more than okay. She trusted her dog's judgment more than she trusted her own. Why did Scout's acceptance of Brian create a flutter of something unfamiliar in her tummy?

"I'll leave the call up to you. But just know I will be having Sera dig into Teresa's back-ground."

"Knock yourself out." Adele opened the slid-ing-glass door and met Teresa's curious look. Refusing to show her upset at the US marshal, Adele plastered a smile on her face and breezed forward. "Are you all done?"

"I am." Teresa stood. Her gaze zeroed in on Brian, who picked up a ball and tossed it for Scout. "Do you want me to hang around?"

"You're sweet to offer. But I promise, all is well." Adele cupped Teresa's elbow and propelled her toward the front door. "I'll contact you when I need you again. However, I'll pay you for the days we miss."

"Wow. Very generous of you." Teresa glanced over her shoulder at Brian, who had stepped back inside. Scout had followed him and now lay on the dog bed in the corner of the living room. To Brian, Teresa said, "It was nice to meet you. I hope you and the judge work out whatever problems you're having." Teresa looked back at Adele and lowered her voice, "Oh. My. Word. He's dreamy. I didn't know you were dating anyone."

A shiver of unexplained excitement worked down Adele's spine. Dating? Hardly. But Brian's words about anyone being a suspect rang in her head. Maybe claiming Brian as her—her what? Certainly not boyfriend. And not a relative. "We're not dating. Like I said, he's just an old friend, here visiting."

"I wouldn't mind an old friend like that visiting me." Teresa laughed as she exited.

Adele shut the door behind her and leaned her forehead against the cool reinforced metal. The house was fortified. Her father had insisted she put in safeguards when she'd had the house built. Did Brian know this? She turned to face him and found him squatted next to where Scout lay flat on his back on his bed, offering up his pink underbelly for the big man to rub. For a moment, she was speechless. Scout barely let her rub his tummy unless it was late at night. She'd never seen Scout in that submissive position with anyone else. "What did you do to my dog?"

"We're becoming friends," Brian told her.

Okay, this day had been beyond strange with a bombing and someone using her for target practice. She should be freaked out and writhing with anxiety. But, like Scout, she felt safe and comforted by Brian's presence. A circumstance neither her nor Scout should get used to.

"I'll get the spare room ready for you."

As she headed down the hall, she berated herself for finding the big man comforting. Not to mention attractive.

Brian watched as Adele restlessly moved about her kitchen. She'd been baking and cooking for two days. One would have thought she was feeding an army with the amount of food she had made as they waited for word from his boss and the San Antonio fire investigators. But so far, no news.

Adele had been on the phone often with her family and her friends, disappearing into her room for long periods of time, which gave him plenty of opportunities to bond with Scout. Though the backyard was fairly small, he would take Scout out periodically and play tug or toss a ball.

The domesticity of being ensconced in Adele's home had Brian antsy, but he'd been trained on many a stakeout how to contain the need to do, to act. He couldn't let boredom or complacency seep in. He had to stay sharp. Alert. That was a problem with Adele constantly humming and looking so cute in yoga pants and a long-sleeved tunic sweater. She was a huge distraction. One he had to figure out how to ignore.

"You're very good with that paring knife," he commented as he leaned against the counter, watching her dice vegetables for a stew she was making.

"After college, but before law school, I did a summer certificate program at the local culinary institute. I thought briefly about becoming a chef. But—" She shrugged.

"The law was calling to you."

She glanced up. For a moment, something arced between them as it did every time their gazes met. Attraction. At least on his part. He was a man with a pulse, and she was a beautiful woman. He'd never lied to himself about finding her appealing from the first moment he'd laid eyes on her two years ago.

But what concerned him was the emotional bonding going on. He didn't do bonding. Or attachment. Too easy to get hurt down that particular path.

He pushed away from the counter and headed for the TV remote. The news reports had been vague about the courthouse bombing, completely leaving out the wounds to the judge and Tomas Garcia. No doubt his boss had pulled some strings at the local stations. Maybe promising them an exclusive once they understood the scope of the situation. "How's your leg?"

"It's healing nicely, thank you. Hardly hurts. I iced it and put some antibacterial ointment over the stitches, like the doctor said to do," she said as she added ingredients to a pot on the stove. "Thankfully, the cut wasn't too deep or too long."

Glad to hear that news, he asked, "And your head?"

"No problem there, either," she told him. "Ice made the bump go away. There's hardly even a sore spot now."

Knowing how close she'd come to being blown to smithereens left him with a disquiet that was slightly assuaged by hearing she wasn't in pain now. If she hadn't bumped her knee on the device beneath the bench, and if she hadn't acted quickly, so many lives could have been extinguished.

Brian's phone rang. He pounced on it, eager for news. Scout trotted over as he answered. The dog put his snout on Brian's knee and Brian absently stroked the dog's head as he answered. "Forrester."

"Deputy Forrester, this is Colleen Jameson from the San Antonio Fire Investigation Unit. Your boss gave me this number and asked that I let you know what we found as we have concluded our investigation into the courthouse bombing."

"I'm all ears." Brian's heart thumped in his chest. Hopefully, they'd found a lead on the bomber. Was this related to the cartel? But if so, why hadn't his boss called him?

"There were, in fact, three devices. One placed under the judge's bench. One under the prosecution table and a third under the defendant's table. All three were remotely detonated."

"The bomber had to be somewhere in the building or just outside." A bold move on the suspect's part. Would the interior security cameras of the courthouse reveal the culprit?

"Not necessarily. From the remnants of the devices, we've ascertained it had a long-range detonation system. The bomber could have been blocks away."

Disappointment shot through him. "Any leads on the bomber?"

"We have gone through an extensive investigation on every person who had access to the courthouse in the days leading up to the bombing. No red flags."

Just because someone didn't have a record didn't mean they were innocent. "But somebody had to get in there to place the bombs. If it wasn't an employee, then who?"

"As I was saying, we found no evidence of foul play by anyone employed by the justice system. And we went through everyone's background with a fine-toothed comb after what happened before."

She was referring to the US marshals' admin who'd been planted in the headquarters by the Garcias. A stain on the US Marshals Service that would take years to scrub away.

"We did, however, discover a glitch in the security cameras on the night before the bombing."

His heart sped up. A major clue. "You could have led with that information."

"I could have, but I wanted you to be aware that the breach in security was not done by anyone employed in the justice system. Whoever planted the explosive devices managed to bypass the security cameras by looping the feed so the security guards were no wiser while the explosives were being planted."

A stunt right out of a movie. "What about CCTV of the surrounding area? Surely there's a camera that caught the perpetrator approaching the courthouse."

"Again, the suspect is good. Like, scary good. They managed to loop every single video camera within a ten-mile radius of the courthouse between the hours of midnight and one o'clock. This is next level hacking."

That didn't bode well for catching him. A deep dread gripped him. "So the guy's good with computers. Was there any forensic evidence left behind?" Even as Brian asked the question, he knew the answer would be no.

"No. The only reason we even discovered the computer video hack was a barely detectable blip in the recording made by one of the security cameras a mile from the courthouse. The camera in question was programmed to reset at 12:15 a.m., which caused a momentary blip in the loop for that camera. And yet, somehow, the hacker was able to capture it and continue the loop. But he couldn't scrub the blip. That, in turn, led us to look more closely at all the security feeds."

Frustration beat a steady beat at his temple. "How do we find this hacker?"

She took an audible breath. "The FBI has had their technicians look at the video feeds and confirm that each video system had been hacked. According to the FBI, there're only a few hackers in the world as good with this kind of capability. This is beyond the scope of the San Antonio Fire Investigation Unit. We've handed the investigation over to the FBI."

Brian gnashed his teeth. The Federal Bureau of Investigation would be highly unlikely to share any of their findings with the marshals service until after they brought down the hacker and bomber. Brian could only pray his boss would figure out a way to play nice with the FBI.

"Thank you for the call." Brian hung up.

Adele moved to stand close to him. "From the hunch of your shoulders, I take it we're no closer to discovering who wants me dead."

"No, we are not. At least, not as far as the

courthouse bombing goes. But I'm going to check in with Sera and Jace and see what they have discovered about our mysterious shooter. He didn't hack the security camera in the hospital parking garage, which is what alerted my boss and Jace."

Brian dialed the marshals service private line for Sera. When she answered, he asked, "Any updates?"

"Well, hello to you, too." Sera's tone held a note of mocking amusement.

He grimaced. "Sorry. I'm frustrated."

Her demeanor sobered. "I take it you heard from the SAFD investigator?"

"I did. What have you discovered on the shooter?"

"Not a lot." Her voice held a derisive pitch. "The white sedan was found outside of town, burned to a crisp. It had been reported stolen two days prior to the shooting. We traced its progress to the hospital from the courthouse. We have video of it entering the parking garage not long after your vehicle. There's footage of the shooting and we catch the sedan again pulling out of the hospital parking garage, but the windows were too heavily tinted to make out the driver. The sedan disappears once again, scrubbed from all video cameras in the city until troopers found the burned remains on a turnout off the highway."

"Must be the same guy who hacked the courthouse security feed. But why did the hacker not loop the hospital security cameras like he did at the courthouse?"

"That's a question we will have to ask him when we find him. But, as of now, we are at a standstill." Her voice held a note of irritation he understood too well.

After a beat, Sera asked, "How's it going there?"

"Good." Brian glanced over his shoulder and watched Adele put a baking sheet of cookies into the oven. Her long red hair hung in a braid down her back and swung as she straightened and turned toward him, her gaze locking with his. So pretty.

He refocused on the phone in his hand. The last thing he needed was to be caught staring and making her aware of his attraction to her. He had to stay professional. Detached. Hard to do in such tight quarters.

Scout went to the back door and sat. A signal that he needed to go out? Brian took the opportunity for privacy, or so he rationalized rather than admit he needed a breather from Adele and headed over to the sliding-glass door and slid it open. The dog bolted outside, Brian followed behind him, shutting the door in his wake. "So how long do you think I'll be here with the judge?"

"I thought you said it was going good?"

Sera's mocking tone grated on his nerves. "It is. But she's getting antsy. And, frankly, so am I." Understatement. He wasn't used to inactivity. He preferred the heightened adrenaline rush of chasing down fugitives, an aspect of the US Marshals Service that he thrived on.

He blew out a breath. "We can't hole up in her home for the rest of our lives. I'm surprised she's let me stay this long." She was soothing herself with constant baking. At this rate, he'd gain ten pounds before this assignment was over. "I wouldn't put it past her to start making noises about going back to work in the next day or so."

"Maybe sooner," Sera said. "There was too much damage at the courthouse to continue to conduct business, so a makeshift courthouse is being set up at an old elementary school."

"Understood." It would be a logistical nightmare. They'd need the cooperation from the city, county and FBI to secure such a venue. "Where's Garcia?"

She snorted. "He's back in jail. His injuries

were minor. Mostly, he'd suffered an angina attack. Got a bad ticker. Who knew?"

Brian didn't want to wish anyone ill but there seemed some poetic justice that Tomas Garcia's heart would cause him problems considering the heartache the man spread through his cartel. "Any headway on locating his illegitimate daughter?"

Sera made a growling noise. "I'm working on it."

Brian didn't doubt that if anyone could locate the woman, it would be Sera. She was a top-notch investigator. He still wondered why she'd chosen the marshals service over FBI or homicide. But he was glad to have her on the team. She brought a certain level of competency and finesse to the job that not many did.

The sliding door opened. Adele filled the doorway. She'd removed the apron. The green, long-sleeved sweater she wore heightened her beauty and made his chest ache.

She arched an eyebrow and said, "Hungry?"

His response came swiftly. "Always."

"She's cooking for you?" Sera's laugh filled his ears. "Yeah, real tough assignment. She's going to spoil you."

He couldn't stop a grin from spreading over

his face and was glad Adele couldn't hear Sera's side of the conversation. "You know it."

"Brian." Sera's voice took on a steely edge. "Make sure you both come out of this situation intact."

"Of course." He turned from Adele and scowled at the fence. "I'm not going to let anything happen to the judge." Sera questioning his abilities grated on his nerves like paws scrabbling across concrete.

"I know you'll keep the judge safe." Her tone suggested he'd offended her. "I'm talking about both of your hearts."

He suppressed a bark of laughter. "You know me, Sera."

"Yes, I do." The adamant confirmation had him sucking in a sharp breath. "Which is why I'm telling you to be careful. You may find it easy to walk away from emotions. But from what little I've gleaned about the judge, not so much. She's had her fair share of trauma."

His heart contracted. What did that mean? Was Sera referring to the courthouse bombing? Or something else? Brian hadn't had time to do his due diligence, which he normally would when taking on a new case subject. "You don't have to worry. Nothing will happen."

He hung up and corralled his irritation and

disquiet. Sera and Jace knew how his chaotic childhood—bouncing from one house to another while a parade of stepparents and stepsiblings came and went—had left Brian jaded on love and commitment. He wasn't about to forget the lessons he'd learned watching his parents and their revolving-door marriages.

Falling for the judge and letting her fall for him wasn't on his agenda. Protecting her was his objective. Nothing more.

SIX

Just as Adele put away the last of the dinner dishes, the front doorbell rang. An anxious burst of alarm revved her pulse. Would panic always be her default mode? Wiping her hands on a towel, she pulled in several calming breaths before heading toward the door.

Brian snagged her elbow, drawing her back against his solid chest. "Let me see who it is first."

"As you wish," she quipped, hoping to belie the rush of adrenaline his touch and his words let loose. Would a bad guy announce his presence?

He arched an eyebrow. Then he grinned and gave her a formal bow.

She appreciated the moment of levity even as her heart thumped with mounting anxiety.

He sobered, a mask of granite dropping over his handsome features as he placed his hand on his holstered weapon and approached the door. He peered out the peephole, stepped back and turned to face her. The expression on his face could only be described as a cross between wariness and dread. "I recognize your parents and sister from the pictures in your living room."

Her heart bumped against her ribs and she gave a small squeal of delight. She rushed past Brian to unlock the door and fling it open. Her father stood proud in his dark navy suit. His salt-and-pepper hair was slicked back from his forehead, revealing his widow's peak. Obviously, he'd recently come from work. Her mother, sitting in her wheelchair, looked lovely in a bright blue pantsuit, her red hair swept up in an artful bun. Behind them was her younger sister, Claire, wearing jeans and a sweatshirt with her college's logo on the front. Her hair, more strawberry-blond than Adele's auburn, was pulled back into a high ponytail, making her appear young and carefree.

Adele flung her arms around her father's neck, breathing in the fresh ocean scent of his aftershave. Then she bent down to kiss her mother's cheek. "I'm so happy to see you all."

"Are you going to invite us inside?" her father asked.

"Of course." She moved back, allowing her mother to wheel herself across the threshold. One of the specifications Adele had made when she'd had the house built was that all the doorways and hallways were extra wide to accommodate her mother.

Her father walked forward and gripped Brian's hand. "Deputy Marshal Forrester, I presume."

Surprise washed over Brian's face. "Yes, sir. Nice to meet you, Mr. Weston."

After an assessing beat, her father said, "Call me Max."

Her mother held out a hand, her diamond wedding ring sparkling in the overhead light. "And I'm Lorraine. We are so thankful you're here to protect our daughter."

Claire moved to stand toe to toe with Brian. Adele suppressed a smile. Her sister had more self-confidence and boldness than most people Adele knew.

Though Claire barely cleared his shoulders, she lifted her chin and skewered Brian with an intense stare. "So you're the man protecting my sister. You don't look like a marshal."

Adele eyed Brian, as well. Except for the holstered gun at his hip, he looked ready to ride the range. The well-worn cowboy boots, denim, and chambray shirt hugging his chest were as appealing as seeing him in a tux had been on that first night when he'd asked her out. She liked both versions of the man standing in front of her. He was a capable protector with experience. Attractive, too, but Adele wouldn't ever say that out loud.

Brian put his right hand up as if taking an oath in court. "I promise I am a marshal."

"We hear they're relocating the court system to Taylor Ferry Elementary School," her father said.

Stunned, Adele wondered how her father knew when she didn't. She cast Brian a glance. His face remained impassive, unreadable. Did he know? "When?"

"Tomorrow, I believe. But you know you can never fully trust the news reports," her mother said. "I assume you'll be going back to work when they do open up?"

"Yes, I will." Adele turned her gaze to Brian. "Did you know about this?"

He had the good grace to flush guiltily. "I learned about it this afternoon."

Irritation flared. "When were you going to tell me?"

His gaze narrowed slightly. "When the time was appropriate."

Adele crossed her arms over her chest. "And just when would you deem it appropriate?"

He flashed her a lopsided grin. She refused to let him affect her, even as her annoyance dimmed.

"Well, now seems as an appropriate time as any," he said with a sheepishness that made her wonder what he was like as a kid. She would imagine his parents had had a hard time corralling him.

Exasperated by her own waning irritation and her affection for him, she turned to her family and sought to change the subject. "I made monster cookies, lemon Bundt cake, crème brûlée, and baked Alaska. What's your pleasure?"

Smiling broadly, her mother's gaze went from Brian to Adele. "It's good you're keeping yourself busy, my dear," her mother said. "I'll take a crème brûlée and a monster cookie."

"Lemon cake for me," her father said as he bent to pet Scout.

"Baked Alaska," Brian said. "I'll help you."

"No, no, no," Claire said. "I'll help." She toggled her fingers at her parents and Brian. "You all get to know each other."

Claire hooked her arm through Adele's and drew her into the kitchen. "I want to hear all about what's been going on."

Adele rolled her eyes. "Nothing has been going on."

"You're baking." Claire released her to grab dishes from the cupboard. "You bake when you're anxious."

"I am anxious." Adele brought the baked Alaska out of the freezer. Figuring her sister already had heard the news about the courthouse bombing, Adele stated flatly, "Someone is trying to blow me up."

"True." Claire gave her a fierce hug. "I thank God they didn't succeed."

"Me, too." She didn't tell her sister about the shooting attempt. Thanks to Brian, the shooter hadn't succeeded. A ribbon of unease wound through her. Would the assassin try again? And when? How? She shivered.

Claire leaned back with worry in her eyes. "Why does someone want you dead?"

The question of the day. Brian had thought it had something to do with Garcia, but Adele couldn't see how that would benefit the man. "I'm sure the marshals will figure it out."

"They'd better." Claire released Adele and moved to the cupboard to grab plates. "I want to know what's going on with you and the good-looking marshal. Is he single?" She waggled her eyebrows. "Do you like him? He's awfully handsome."

Rolling her eyes to keep from revealing her feelings to her sister, Adele said, "Let's just get the desserts going."

She would never confess to her sister that she'd been cooking up a storm not because of her normal anxiety, made exponentially worse by the attempts on her life, but because of the too handsome man underfoot. Contrary to his statement that she'd hardly know he was there, her awareness of him was acute. Perhaps getting back to work would alleviate her anxiety and her attraction to a certain cowboy marshal.

The old elementary school on the outskirts of town was set back from the main road. A large field that needed to be mowed stretched behind the school and, beyond the field, a grove of oak trees grew thick and tall. The building itself was nothing to look at. Long, U-shaped wings with rectangular windows framed a central courtyard. Several of the larger classrooms had been commandeered and converted into makeshift courtrooms.

Brian prowled along the bank of windows, some cracked open to let in some fresh air, in the classroom assigned to Adele as her provisional courtroom. He didn't like the various hiding spots that could conceal a shooter. The trees in the distance could provide a seasoned sniper a roost easily enough.

The responsibility to keep Adele out of harm's way carried more weight than normal. He always took his job of protection seriously, but with Adele…they'd become friends and he liked the woman beneath the black judge's robe. Seeing her today in her official role made him realize she used the robe as a shield. A way to distance herself from others, which he supposed was part of her job.

Brian didn't like how exposed Adele was, sitting at the front of the room. He kept an eye out the windows for any glint of a scope on a sniper rifle. Nobody could get within a hundred feet of the school and a perimeter of armed officers stood guard, but that wouldn't stop someone from climbing a tree in the distance. With some skill and the right equipment… Just because the shooter had failed his mission outside the hospital didn't mean he wouldn't try again.

Brian sent up a silent plea to God that nothing would happen to put Adele in danger.

He told himself his worry over her safety was purely professional. He refused to let his respect and admiration for Adele turn into something more. He needed to stay detached, professional. Do his job. Stay focused.

She sat at what would have been the teacher's desk and was giving a speech about the responsibility of jury duty. Scout lay at her feet. She wouldn't leave him at home alone and had insisted he come with her. A bit unorthodox, but then again, they were in an elementary school holding court.

Student desks had been arranged into three rows with an aisle running through the middle. A new set of potential jurors dotted the room, crammed into the too-small-for-adults desks. Many of the jurors who had been in the courtroom when it had exploded had declined to return on the grounds of post-traumatic stress. He certainly didn't blame them.

Brian wished Adele would claim some post-traumatic stress, given how close she'd come to being blown up and then shot, but she was determined to carry on.

The defense attorney had already stated that Tomas Garcia had refused to return for the jury selection process. The man still insisted he'd been the intended target of the bomb and, despite their assurance he wasn't in danger, Tomas was certain another attempt would be made either on him or on the judge, and he didn't want to be anywhere near a courtroom.

Adele's clerk, Jordan, entered the room and hurried to the desk-turned-bench, an envelope in his hand. She put her hand over the microphone while he spoke into her ear.

Frowning, Brian wanted to know what was so urgent that the clerk would interrupt her. She said something and the clerk nodded then headed toward the back of the room, where he took a seat. Jordan opened the envelope in his hand, releasing a puff of white powder into the air. The clerk coughed and waved his hand to disperse the particles.

Alarm bells banged in Brian's head. "Jordan, put down the envelope and move to the window. Everyone else out!"

"What's going on?" Jordan asked, his voice shaking and panic rising in his expression.

Not wanting to alarm the young man, Brian refrained from voicing his suspicions. "I don't know yet, but I'm not taking any chances." He motioned for everyone to hurry through the exit.

Closing the distance to Adele's side, he grabbed her, practically lifted her from her seat and propelled her out the closest exit. Scout stayed at Adele's side, his leash in her hand.

"Did you touch the envelope?" he asked her.

"What?" She stared up at him in alarm. "The one Jordan had? No. Why?"

Brian moved them far from the room. He called Jace, who was standing guard with Sera at the entrance to the school. "We've got a situation."

Brian told Jace what he suspected. "White powdery substance. Could be nothing. Could be something dangerous. Airborne."

Beside him, Adele gasped. "Oh, no."

"On our way," Jace told him.

Brian waved to another of the court security guards. "Get a hazmat team here, stat."

More security guards hustled forward from their posts around the school as word spread that something was happening.

"We need to evacuate the school. Everybody into the courtyard," Brian instructed.

Jace and Sera joined him. "We've got this," Jace said. "You secure the judge."

Instead of joining the rest of the people in the courtyard, he hustled her out the front door to the SUV he'd borrowed from his boss. He wasn't taking any chances with her safety.

"We can't just leave," she protested. "I'm in the middle of court proceedings."

Brian opened the passenger door and urged her inside. "Proceedings are over for today."

He then secured Scout in the back passenger seat.

A siren filled the air as an ambulance roared to a halt in front of the school. Brian was glad to see the quick response time. He sent up a prayer that the paramedics reached Jordan in time to halt whatever poison had been in the envelope.

When they were on the road heading back to the judge's neighborhood, he asked, "What did Jordan say to you when he came up to the bench?"

"Someone handed him an envelope and told him it was urgent for me to see what was inside." She gasped and put a hand to her throat. "That envelope was meant for me?"

His gut churned with apprehension. This had been another attempt on her life. "Yes, it was. Whatever was inside is probably poisonous."

"But Jordan…" She looked like she might be sick.

He released one hand from the steering wheel to reach for hers. "He'll get the help he needs. My job is to protect you."

He couldn't believe the killer had managed to get so close. Who had handed Jordan the envelope? How had they gotten past the wall of security surrounding the elementary school? His hand tightened on the steering wheel while the petal-soft feel of her palm pressed against his other hand seared him to the core.

Somebody was going to pay when he found out who the traitor was among those sworn to protect.

After calling to ensure Sera and Jace had access to the State of Texas court records to acquire the judge's case files from her time as both a prosecutor and a judge, Brian patrolled the house, securing all the windows and doors. Adele had retreated to her room. Scout sat at the back door, every now and then giving a little whine.

Relenting, Brian opened the door and let the dog out. Scout went around to the side of the house while Brian walked the fence line.

Scout brought his ball and dropped it at Brian's feet. He picked up the ball and tossed it. Scout ran across the grass to the edge of the fence. The dog picked up the ball, paused, then dropped it to sniff the ground around the fence. A few seconds later, a feline head appeared over the top of the fence. Scout barked as the cat scampered across the top rail and disappeared into the neighbor's yard.

"At least we know you will keep her safe from any critters."

Brian threw the ball a few more times for Scout before heading back inside to pace the living room. Scout jumped onto the couch, his big paws hanging over the edge and his head resting on the arm. His dark eyes watched Brian.

Adele came out of her bedroom. She'd changed from her work clothes and into bright red sweats. The bottoms of which had the words Corpus Christi up the side of one pant leg. The matching hooded sweat jacket had a screen print of the Corpus Christi beach. Her auburn hair had been set loose to brush over her shoulders. So pretty.

She asked, "Any word on Jordan?"

"Last update I received was that he was being treated for anthrax poisoning. But his prognosis is good. His exposure was minimal."

She stopped midstride, her hands fisting at her sides. "Who did this?"

"Someone very determined," Brian replied. "Jace and Sera are bringing your old case files that haven't been digitized for us to comb through."

Adele sat on the couch, drawing her bare feet beneath her. "A fun stroll down memory lane. Not."

Joining her on the couch, he sought to keep her mind from the horror of being a target. "Do you spend much time at the beach?"

"I do," she replied. "Every summer, growing up, my family headed south. The water's warm on my feet, the sun hot, and there's freedom to just run up and down the shoreline. I haven't had a chance to take Scout there yet."

"Sounds like you have good memories. I'm sure Scout will love the ocean. I must admit I prefer the Texas beaches over the California ones. Both are beautiful in their own ways, though."

"Did you surf while you were in California?"

"Yep. The coastline from San Diego to the northern part of the state offers every type of wave you can imagine. I've surfed here in Texas, too. But the best waves here are in the winter months, and I prefer warm water."

She smiled softly. "You're a good swimmer then."

"I am. My grandparents bought a house on Medina Lake, where I spent a lot of time with my cousins when not at school or some summer camp or visiting one of my parents. Swimming was a must."

Her brows drew together. "You grew up around here?"

"Born and raised here," Brian told her. "My parents divorced when I was five." Memories assailed him, and he pushed them back. "My dad moved to Ohio. I spent a fair amount of time up north. My mom stayed around here."

At least he'd go but not stay long. His father hadn't been too interested in having his son around. Too busy with whatever woman he was with at the time.

Sympathy darkened her pretty, amber-colored eyes. "It had to have been tough on you at such a young age for your father to move away. Did you fly back and forth?"

"Sometimes. They both moved often. And sometimes my mom would drive me halfway and Dad would pick me up. My parents both went through several new spouses, some with kids, and both produced siblings that are scattered around."

The empathy written in her expression tightened his gut. "Hard to become attached to anyone?"

"Yes, it is." No one could be counted on to fully commit which was exactly why he didn't do serious relationships. He wasn't going to end up like his parents.

After a moment, she asked, "Why did you join the marshals service?"

Brian stretched his arm across the back of the couch. This was a more favorable topic to discuss. "I met Jace when I was fourteen. His family would come to the lake during breaks." He smiled, remembering. "I was fascinated with the idea of the US Marshals Service. Jace would always complain that his dad was never home. But I saw how committed his father was to the service and to his family." Admiration and respect had grown over the years for Gavin. "When Gavin was around, he was all-in."

Acid burned in Brian's veins. "Unlike my own father. There were times when I went to visit my dad and he didn't even realize I was there."

Adele reached across the space between them to briefly touch his leg. "I'm sorry that happened to you."

With just the slightest move, his stretched arm could be around her shoulders. The yearning to pull her close had his skin itching. He removed his arm from the top of the couch and smoothed his hands down his thighs, as if he could smooth away his attraction.

"It is what it is," he remarked. He didn't want pity. Life happened. Everyone had troubles. He was no exception. "Anyway, when I graduated high school, I applied to the San Antonio Police Department. Four years later, Jace applied. We both served on SAPD for a couple years."

"Then you decided to go to the marshals service together?"

He chuckled. "Funny enough, we each made the decision to apply without telling the other. I thought he'd be mad because his father was a marshal. And Jace thought I'd feel like he was abandoning me."

She tucked a strand of hair behind her ear. "Sounds as though you guys have a deep friendship."

He caught a whiff of her floral scent. She smelled like a meadow and sunshine. An ache settled in his chest. "The deepest. We were both stunned and immensely happy to discover that we both got into the same class. We met Sera there."

"You three work well together."

Her observation pleased him. "We do. We have a lot in common."

"Like being dedicated. And good at your job."

Surprised at her praise, warmth spread through him. She sounded like she admired him. Like she cared. But there were more ways he, Jace and Sera were alike.

"And commitment shy," he blurted before he

could stop himself. He winced at the revealing statement. He wasn't usually so self-aware but remembering Sera's admonishment to keep his and Adele's heart safe seemed to have made an impact.

Adele tilted her head, her gaze curious and confused. "I thought I heard someone mention Jace was married?"

That had been astounding to Brian. "He is and has a baby on the way. I couldn't be happier for them." Thinking of how different Jace was after falling in love with Abby, Brian said, "Jace changed for the better. Marriage seemed to have settled down his restlessness."

Adele was silent for a long moment. What was going on in her beautiful mind? Did she share the same commitment-phobic tendencies as him? Or was she searching for a fairy-tale romance? She was a beautiful woman. Why was she single? What kept her from finding love? But the bigger question was why did he care?

SEVEN

Brian thought she was done with the conversation, which was fine by him, but then she said, "Staying in the marshals service seems like a big commitment to me. You are dedicated to your job."

His insides stilled. "I am committed to my work. But a different kind of commitment is required in a romantic relationship."

She held his gaze, her eyes seeming to search for something in him that he wasn't sure was there. "You've never been tempted to commit to a romantic relationship?"

Growing uncomfortable with the conversation, Brian forced himself to stay seated when he really wanted to move away from the question. "No. I've dated. Casually."

"And Sera?"

"She has her own reasons for staying unattached and hasn't cared to share all of them. I think that's why we all get along so well. We would do anything for each other. But we all know where the boundary is when it comes to all that touchy-feely kind of stuff."

"Touchy-feely?" Adele laughed, but the sound rang hollow. "I get that."

His curiosity piqued, he asked, "How so?"

She glanced up, meeting his eyes. "You don't know?"

Something niggled at the back of his brain. It seemed like he should know something. He'd read up on the judge two years ago when he'd first noticed her, but nothing had popped out at him to suggest something that would cause her to be commitment phobic. Her bouts of anxiety must stem from whatever had happened in her past. He should've taken the time to do a thorough background check when his boss had tasked him with this assignment, except there hadn't been time at the beginning and, since then, he hadn't felt the need.

Though, honestly, he'd rather hear the story directly from her than read it in some report. "I know you're young to be a judge. I know you spent four years as a prosecutor. I know you graduated top of your class. What am I missing?"

She was silent so long, he didn't think she

would open up. Then, in a soft voice, she said, "I was assaulted my first year of college."

A burst of anger shot through his system. He sat straighter. His hands clenched. Someone had abused this kind and compassionate woman?

Before Brian could ask Adele for details about the assault she'd suffered in college, there was a knock at the front door. He ground his teeth at the intrusion. He wanted her to confide in him. Though why, he couldn't have said exactly. To help with the case? To give him a better understanding of how to protect her? Or because he wanted to be trusted? To be included in her inner-most secrets?

Definitely because it would help with the case. He couldn't let things get too personal.

She tensed. "Your friends?"

He hoped so. "Only one way to find out." He stood, rolling the tension from his shoulder.

Adele rose, as well, and moved to let Scout out the back sliding-glass door.

Brian went to the front door, peered through the peephole to affirm it was indeed his friends, then yanked the door open. Sera and Jace each held the handle of a folding hand truck stacked high with bankers boxes. "Your timing is impeccable, as always."

He gestured at the boxes. "Is that all of it?"

Jace pushed his load forward, forcing Brian to step back to allow Jace and Sera to enter. He parked the hand truck on the marble floor and scooted the boxes off.

"Nope. Two more loads." Jace turned to Adele, who now stood at the entrance to the kitchen. "Good afternoon, Judge Weston."

"Deputy Marshal Armstrong," Adele replied. She turned her gaze to Sera. "Deputy Marshal Morales."

"Call me Sera, he's Jace." She scooted her stack of boxes off the hand truck next to Jace's stack. "No need to stand on formality when we're making work for you."

Brian noticed a shiver run through Adele. He had to fight the urge to take her into his arms. Why did the need to comfort her come so easily?

"It will be worth the effort if we can figure out who wants me dead," Adele said. "And, please, call me Adele."

Brian focused on his friends and colleagues. "Did you figure out how the envelope got past security and into Jordan's hands?"

Jace nodded, a grim look crossing his face. "A courier dropped it off."

"I found the courier service," Sera said. "And talked to the courier. He picked it up from one of Senator Ortega's aides."

"What?" Adele's shocked voice reverberated through Brian. "John sent it?"

Brian's jaw clenched. He thought back to the way the senator had hovered over Adele after the bombing. "Do we really believe the senator is behind the attempts on Adele?"

Brian hadn't sensed any undercurrent of animosity when Ortega had interacted with Adele at the courthouse. Possessiveness yes, but not malice.

"Too soon to tell," Sera replied. "The boss is taking a run at Ortega."

Adele shook her head. "John wouldn't do this. He's a friend."

Brian was sure the senator wanted to be more than just a friend to Adele, but he kept that to himself. "Senator Ortega wouldn't be careless enough to have an aide hire a courier that could be traced back to his office if his intent was to harm Adele. It's a setup."

Adele smiled at him with approval, and his breath caught in his throat. He liked pleasing her way too much.

"Thank you," Adele said. "I've known John for a long time. He wouldn't hurt me."

Aware of Jace's and Sera's gazes, Brian said, "I don't like the senator, but his concern for you after the courthouse bombing did seem genuine."

An emotion flittered across her face before

her expression changed into a polite smile as she turned to Jace and Sera. "I've fresh cookies, lemon cake and baked Alaska. Would you like a treat?"

"All of the above, please," Sera said with a grin. "Let's get the rest of these in here first." As Sera passed Brian, she patted him on the arm on her way out of the house. "Not a bad gig at all."

"I'll help them," Brian told Adele as he followed Jace out the door, closing it softly behind him. He hustled to the back of the SUV and grabbed the closest box to place it on Sera's dolly. "You guys need to behave yourselves. The judge is a lady and deserves respect."

"Boy, you've got it bad," Jace said with a grin.

"Look at his face turn red," Sera joked, but her gaze wasn't amused.

Remembering Sera's warning about not hurting the judge emotionally, Brian held up his hands. "Stop it. This is an assignment like any other."

"One you didn't want," Sera shot back.

"I don't need you to keep reminding me of that."

"Why didn't you want this assignment, exactly?" Jace asked, the picture of innocence.

Brian ignored the heat rising up his neck again. "I have just as much of an interest in dismantling the Garcia cartel as you two."

Sera shrugged. "If you want, I can stay with

the judge, and you can go off with Jace to find the Montoya woman."

A protest rose within Brian and he clamped his lips shut before he could let it escape. No way did he want his friends to know just how unwilling he was to give up this assignment, despite his initial reluctance. He'd grown fond of Adele and had promised her he'd protect her.

He turned on his heels and carried a box to the house. The door opened and this time Scout darted outside, dancing around Sera and Jace. Brian whistled and the dog came running back to his side.

"Great, he's going to obey you instead of me," Adele said from the open doorway. "I can barely get him to sit."

Brian gave a shrug. "We can work on your obedience training."

She cocked an eyebrow. "Don't you mean Scout's obedience training?"

"More often than not, a dog's disobedience is due to the owner or handler. Scout's smart. He knows how to push you around."

Giving a little huff, Adele disappeared to the kitchen. Brian turned to find Jace and Sera staring at him. They exchanged a glance rife with meaning that had Brian's insides twisting. He led the way to the living room.

Adele came out of the kitchen, carrying two plates laden with a slice of each of her delectable desserts. "You can sit at the dining table."

"We'll take those to go, if you don't mind?" Jace said with a glance at Brian. "We should let you two get to the business of searching for who might be trying to harm you."

Without a word, Adele nodded and returned a moment later with both plates wrapped in foil. "You can return the plates next time I see you."

Sera took the plates and stepped closer to Adele. "If you need to talk, woman to woman, don't hesitate to call me. Brian has my number. It's these kinds of situations where your life is in danger when it's good to talk to somebody who—" Sera gave a shake of her head. "In our line of work, we've all had close calls."

The grateful expression on Adele's face had Brian's heart squeezing tight. Maybe he should let Sera stay. But he couldn't bring himself to do it. And, if pressed, he wouldn't have been able to explain with any believable rationale.

After Sera and Jace left, Brian shut the door and locked it.

Adele picked up the top box from one of the dollies and headed for the coffee table. "Might as well get to work."

* * *

Sitting on the floor with file folders and empty boxes surrounding her, Adele let out a huge sigh of frustration. She and Brian had been at this for hours. They'd come up with a list of ten people so far who might not only have a grudge against her but also the personality to act on it. Locating each one and seeing if they were anywhere in the area at the time of the bombing and the shooting would take time, though.

Her back ached from sitting on the floor. She got up and stretched. The world tilted as blood rushed from her head. Quickly, she flopped onto the couch and put her head between her knees. A wave of nausea hit her, sending the scallops and fettuccine she'd made for dinner bobbing in her stomach. Thankfully, she didn't throw up.

A warm hand landed on her back, drawing little circles of comfort. "You okay?"

"No. I've got a horrible headache. Sick to my stomach and dizzy. This doesn't feel like a panic attack, though. This is different."

The hand on her back stopped. "I've got a headache, too. And I'm a bit queasy."

Adele's gaze shot to where Scout lay on his bed, his tongue lolling out the side of his mouth and his eyes rolled back.

Adele gasped. Alarm flared white-hot. "Something's wrong. Look at Scout."

In a flurry of movement, Brian stood, braced his feet apart as if to keep from toppling over. Then he hooked an arm under hers and helped her to her feet. For a moment, she swayed like she had the time she and her sister had gone on a Disney cruise and a wake in the ocean had rocked the ship.

"We need to get out of here." Brian led her to the back door and slid it open.

Fresh air rushed in, along with clarity. "Carbon monoxide."

"My thought, too." Brian scooped Scout into his arms and followed Adele onto the back patio. For long moments, they both gulped in air. Soon, Scout roused, wanting to be let down. He stood facing the sliding-glass door and barked.

"I'm sure I didn't leave the gas stove on," Adele said, the distress of having made such a horrible mistake flooding through her. But she had to admit she'd been distracted as she'd prepared their meal.

Earlier today, someone had tried to poison her with anthrax and instead had ended up hurting her clerk. Then she'd overheard Brian's coworker, Sera, offer to stay in place of

Brian. Adele couldn't deny she'd been grateful when he'd declined switching places.

Not that she had anything against Sera. She was sure the US marshal was competent and would be a great friend, but Brian made her feel safe. And he knew her secret about her panic attacks.

She could feel the anxiety fluttering low in her belly and moving up into her chest. But she fought off the wave of anxiousness with slow, steady breaths. Having Brian close helped to keep her calm.

"I don't think this is a gas leak from the stove," Brian said. "I'll call the gas company. I'm going back in to get my phone."

"I can do it," she offered, though she didn't want to. But she didn't want to be responsible for any harm befalling Brian, either.

He gave her an incredulous look. "You and Scout stay here where it's safe. In fact, I'd like you both to move over to the far corner, away from the house."

Fresh alarm clanged in her pounding head. "Do you think the house will explode?"

"I hope not." For a moment, he stood staring at the house. "Come on. We're going around to the front through the back gate."

He hustled her and Scout around the side of the house, past the garbage cans, to the gate leading to the front yard. He propelled her to the sidewalk. "Do you know your neighbors?"

"I know the Hinsons who live across the street." She pointed to the two-story house. "The house lights are on."

Grabbing her by the elbow, he propelled her across the street and onto the Hinsons' front porch. He wrapped his knuckles on the big door. From inside the house, music ceased and the sound of footsteps approached the door.

Harrison Hinson opened the door. Slim and fit for a man his age, his eyes widened with obvious surprise. "Judge Weston. Is something wrong?"

"There is." Brian flashed his badge at the man. "We need to use your phone."

Harrison stepped back, allowing them entrance. Brian told Scout to stay. The dog lay down on the welcome mat as if guarding the exit.

Adele had never been inside her neighbor's home. She'd only waved at the Hinsons from the driveway. Their house was much more ostentatious than her own, and not nearly as fortified. The front door was not made of metal but of solid wood painted a cheerful red. The entryway was large, with slate floors, and to the right was a big dining room with pillars holding up the ceiling. She could see at the end of the long corridor a beautifully appointed kitchen.

Tamara Hinson walked out of the kitchen archway, wiping her hands on a towel. She was a petite woman with jet-black hair that hung down her back. Her curious gaze raked over Brian then turned to Adele. "This is unexpected. Judge Weston, is everything okay?"

"He's a US marshal," Harrison said with an excited buzz in his voice. "He needs to use the phone."

"Of course. Right this way." Tamara led them through a set of double doors into a large office. "This is Harrison's private domain." She laughed. "He works from home." She gestured to the landline attached to the desk. "Help yourselves."

Brian strode forward to use the phone. Adele glanced at Harrison and Tamara. "Could you give us a moment?" She didn't want them to panic if there was no cause. She hoped there was a reasonable explanation for the gas leak.

The couple nodded and quickly retreated, closing the double doors behind them. Adele moved closer to Brian as he talked in a low voice to whomever was on the line. "Yes, I think a gas valve has been opened or cut under the house. We need the gas company to come out. Tell them to be low-key. We don't want to alarm the neighbors."

He hung up. "Once the gas company turns the gas off and the house is cleared, you're going to pack a bag. We need to find a safe place that no one knows about."

"A US marshal safe house?"

"No. I've something better in mind." He ushered her out the door of the office and nearly ran into the Hinsons. Clearly, they'd been trying to overhear their conversation. Adele couldn't muster up any annoyance. She'd be curious, too, if someone had barged into her house wanting to use the phone at dinnertime. She grasped Tamara's hands. "Thank you so much for letting us use your phone. I really appreciate it."

"Any time," Tamara said.

Adele and Brian headed to the front door.

"Does this have anything to do with the bombing at the courthouse?" Harrison asked.

"Sorry, it's classified," Brian told him.

"We also heard about the incident at the elementary school. Is someone out to get you?" Tamara questioned.

Brian studied the two, making them visibly squirm. Adele touched his arm and shook her head. He couldn't suspect the Hinsons of being the culprits, could he? What reason would they want her dead?

"Thank you for your hospitality," Brian said

and ushered Adele out the door. Scout rose from his spot on the stoop and trotted alongside as they walked to the gate at the front of the complex to wait.

Two US marshals' vehicles roared up to the gate with the gas company truck and the fire department not far behind. Adele put in her code and the metal gate opened. Brian talked to Jace, who drove the first Suburban, before leading the others down her street, stopping two houses away from her house.

The gas company workers climbed out of their truck and jogged over, at the same time the fire crew joined them. Brian explained about being nauseous and dizzy while inside the house. "I left the back slider open."

"Good call," the elder of the two gas company men said. "Any spark in the house could ignite the gas. We need to get everybody in the surrounding homes evacuated and at least three hundred feet from the judge's house."

The fire crew and the gas company employees went to work to secure the house.

Adele's breathing escalated. She'd put everyone on her block in jeopardy. How many more people would she endanger before this was over?

EIGHT

Adele stayed close to Brian as he related their situation to the four people who'd climbed out of the marshals' SUVs.

"We need to get everyone in the area to gather near the community gate," Marshal Gavin Armstrong said. He turned to the other deputy standing nearby. "Conlan, you keep order at the gate. Brian and I will coordinate with the fire crew and the gas company."

"Yes, sir." Deputy Conlan walked back to the gate to talk to the gathering crowd.

Sera and Jace hustled off, as well, each taking a side of the street and knocking on doors. Gavin headed for the fire truck.

"You need to wait at the gate with your neighbors," Brian told Adele.

"Only if you come with me," she replied, unwilling to let him put himself in harm's way for her sake. She didn't want to admit that having him near made her feel safer.

"I need to talk to the gas company to make sure your house is clear," he said, already turning away from her. "But you and Scout need to go"

Irritation swamped her, ratcheting up the anxiety threatening to overwhelm her. "Don't dismiss me. You either come or I stay."

Swiftly, he focused on her. "Think of Scout, if not yourself."

He played dirty. Of course, she didn't want Scout to get hurt. "Fine. I'll take Scout to the gate."

And then she would head right back to his side. She marched off and stopped a few feet away when she realized Scout hadn't moved from Brian. Even the dog wanted to stay with him. Didn't the frustrating man realize… Realize what?

She didn't know and right now was not the time or place to analyze all the emotions crowding her mind and her heart. Brian didn't even have on a hazard suit like the gas company men or the firefighters.

If the house exploded, he could be injured— she tamped down that thought. She snapped her fingers, drawing Scout's attention. "Come."

The dog started for her but then hesitated and glanced up at Brian. He bent down and whispered in the dog's ear. Straightening, he made a hand motion like he was sending the dog off. And Scout trotted to her side.

Adele made a face at Brian then at Scout. "You little traitor."

The dog licked her hand.

Affection filled her chest. "Okay, fine, you're forgiven."

She and Scout hustled off to join the other neighbors at the entrance gate to the community. The US marshals were trying to calm everyone down. But the upset residents peppered the marshals with questions. These people were worse than the paparazzi. Marshal Armstrong and the fire chief joined in trying to assure the group they had the situation under control.

She approached Gavin. "Marshal, can I address my neighbors?"

Gavin scrubbed a hand down his whiskered chin and gave a nod. "It might help. Just be careful how much you reveal. We don't want a full-on panic."

"I understand." Adele pushed past the marshal and wove her way through the crowd. She stepped up on one of the concrete pillars holding the sides of the gate up. She raised a hand.

"Please, if you all could just take a breath and listen to me."

"What's going on?" someone yelled out.

"Does this have to do with the bombing at the courthouse?"

"Or the incident at the school?"

"What's happening?"

"Why is the gas company and the fire department here?"

Understanding how scary this must be, Adele raised her voice to be heard over the voices. "Please, listen. We don't have answers. I'm sure I most likely left one of the gas valves open and it filled the house. My mistake."

"Well, that was dumb," somebody groused.

"Yes, it was," she shouted back. "A little grace here would be really nice."

The crowd's mumblings died down. Jace Armstrong held out his hand and helped her off the concrete pylon. She hadn't even noticed that Jace, Sera and Gavin had joined them at the gate. He ushered her to his boss.

"You didn't have to take the heat for this," Gavin said.

"Sure, she did," Sera said. "Going on the offensive is the best way to handle a scared crowd."

Adele smiled at the other woman. She liked her. "Thank you."

Sera gave her a nod. "Here comes Brian."

Adele's instinct was to rush up to him and make sure he was okay. Or rather, that her house was okay. She forced herself to stay rooted to the ground.

"Report?" Gavin asked Brian.

Brian met Adele's gaze. "The gas has all dissipated. A portable gas heater in the crawl space beneath the house had been left on."

"What?" Dread gripped Adele's chest. "I don't own a space heater. And even if I did, I certainly wouldn't have it under the house."

"There's no telling how long ago it was left there," Brian said. "Once the gas filled the crawl space, it rose, which is why we became ill."

Adele's stomach dropped. Who had access to her house to the extent they could go underneath and place a gas heater?

Only a few people came to mind. Her dog sitter was one. But why would Teresa want to harm her or Scout? There had to be another explanation. "I have a cleaning service that comes once a month. But they've cleaned my house since I moved in, and it's been a couple of weeks since they were last out." Surely, if one of them had left the gas heater in the crawl space, she'd have felt the effect long before tonight.

"We'll check into them," Gavin said.

"Boss, can I talk to you?" Brian tugged Gavin out of earshot.

Adele feared there was more to the story but Brian didn't want her to know what it was. She hated being left in the dark. She hated even more the thought that Teresa, a woman she trusted with her dog, was involved in trying to hurt her.

As soon as Brian had Gavin far enough away from Adele to be sure she wouldn't hear their conversation, he said to his boss, "That was a close call. Not an hour before, Adele had been cooking."

His stomach twisted, thinking of all the times she'd turned on the gas stove or baked something delicious in the last few days. Horrible images of her burned and in agony seared his brain. Sweat broke out at his nape. He reined in his thoughts to focus.

Gavin put his hand on Brian's shoulder. "It doesn't do anyone any good to conjure up the worst-case scenario when Adele is safe now."

"Right." Brian took a breath that eased the constriction in his chest. "I asked Sera to check into Teresa Watts, the dog sitter, but nothing came up to indicate she could be behind the attempts on the judge's life. I need to do an even deeper dive. Question her and see if she let anyone into the house or onto the property that she'd failed to mention to Adele."

"Sera can do it. You and the judge aren't going to be staying here. We'll put you both up in a hotel."

Brian shook his head. "I'd rather take her out to my family's lake house. The place is not in my name. It wouldn't be easy for anyone to connect me to the property. Nobody would find her there."

"If someone is determined enough…" Gavin said.

Brian understood. There were no guarantees in life. Everyone in law enforcement knew there were risks and knew criminals were hard to stop when bent on destruction. "It would be easier to protect her in the country than in a hotel downtown."

"I don't have a problem with you taking her out of the city," Gavin said. "But I want Deputy Conlan to go with you."

"I'd appreciate the backup."

Having the other deputy along would also provide a needed buffer between him and Adele. Because Brian was having a difficult time keeping his emotions in check where the lovely judge was concerned.

* * *

The preparations to move Adele to Brian's family's lake house commenced without a hiccup, much to Brian's satisfaction, but he didn't breathe easy until two hours later. After a stop at the 24-hour grocery store for supplies, he turned into the circular drive of his grandparents' lake house.

The two-story home with a wide porch in front and a large deck in back sat at the tip of a small peninsula on Medina Lake. The backside of the house looked out over the water and covered dock, housing kayaks and a motorized speedboat.

The sun rose high in the early morning and light sparkled on the water. There were a few fishermen already out in aluminum fishing boats, hoping to catch a bass or catfish.

Beside him, Adele leaned forward in the passenger seat of his personal rig, a dark green sport utility vehicle.

"The US Marshals Service owns this?"

The awe in her voice made him smile. "No. My grandparents built this house in the '50s. The whole family uses it as a vacation home. You can see cars coming from a mile away. The only other way to access the house is from the lake."

She stared at him. "I'm honored you'd bring me here. It's lovely."

Pleased by her words, he held her gaze. "Wait until you see the inside."

He liked the way her eyes lit up. She was so pretty and kind. Smart and brave. For some reason, Brian was excited to show Adele the house. He and his cousins had put a lot of manual labor into updating the amenities. This house had been his sanctuary as a kid and would now be one for Adele. He was glad he could provide that for her.

Because it was his job.

Deputy Joe Conlan brought his own SUV to a halt beside Brian's.

Brian cleared his throat. "We should go in."

Grabbing their bags and the grocery sacks, he escorted her and Scout to the porch.

"Wow, this is awesome," the younger deputy said as he jogged over with his to-go bag in hand.

Brian gave Conlan one of the grocery bags as he unlocked the front door.

Adele sent one of the rocking chairs sitting on the porch to rocking with a gentle push. Scout sniffed along the edge of the porch. "I can imagine sitting here drinking coffee in the morning and looking out over the hills."

Brian turned to follow her scrutiny of the tree-dotted landscape. The rolling greenery with natural foliage stretched for as far as the eye could see. It was a soothing site. "We have rocking chairs on the back porch, as well. You'll be comfortable and safe."

"Thank you for thinking of this place and allowing me to stay here."

"Of course." He opened the door so she could step inside. Scout slipped past and Brian followed them inside the lake house.

"This is beautiful," Adele said as she turned slowly around, taking it all in.

For some reason, it gave him immense pleasure to be sharing this place with her. Hardwood floors stretched beneath their feet. A large stone fireplace dominated one end of the great room. Comfortable couches and chairs had been arranged for conversation and to take advantage of the view through the floor-to-ceiling windows and sliding-glass door that opened onto the back deck.

"Where am I bunking?" Conlan asked from behind Brian.

Swinging his attention from Adele, Brian gestured to a closed door. "Joe, you'll be staying in this room here. One of my uncles uses this when he comes to stay."

Joe opened the door and squeezed past him through the doorway into the bedroom. "Nice. This is great." Conlan walked to the bedroom window facing the front of the house. "Good vantage point to keep an eye on the road."

Brian nodded and dipped out of the room, leaving Conlan to settle in. Each room in the house had its own bathroom. One of the many upgrades he and his cousins had made over the last few years. Though he noted a few additional changes that he hadn't been a part of while he'd been in California. Someone had changed out the Formica kitchen countertop for granite.

Adele had moved to the door leading out to the back deck. Scout sat beside her. "This is amazing."

Sunlight glinted off her hair in fiery sparks. Her ability to adapt to and handle whatever was thrown at her despite her anxiety was admirable. The more time he spent with her, the more he found to like about her. She was amazing. And set his heart to pounding.

Giving himself a mental head shake, he gestured to the stairs at the end of the great room and said, "Let me show you to your room."

At the top of the stairs was a large loft where several bean bag chairs littered the floor, a gaming console took up space in the corner with a large-screen TV, and bookcases with books and a window seat for reading made the space cozy.

"My cousins all have kids," Brian explained. "When they come to the lake house, this is usually where the preteens and teens end up." Back in his day, there were video games, only a small TV, books and board games.

She smiled at him. "I can see why they would."

He returned the smile and ushered her down a short hall to another en suite. It was the largest in the house and was decorated in soothing blues with white oak furniture. "This is my grandparents' room when they are here."

Hesitating in the doorway, she said, "Are you sure it's okay for me to use the room?"

"I'm sure." He was also confident his grandparents would love her. Not that his family would meet her. They weren't a couple or anything close to being romantically involved. She was an assignment. Though why he had to remind himself of the fact jabbed at him like an annoying finger in the back.

Suddenly overheating, he tugged at the collar of his shirt. "You should find everything you need in the bathroom. I'll be downstairs in a room almost directly beneath you if you need anything." He set her bags down on the floor and backed away.

She ran a hand along the beautiful wood dresser. "Whoever decorated this home did a lovely job."

He had to agree. "That would be my mom and my aunts."

Adele approached the four-poster then turned to look at him. "I need to apologize."

He tucked in his chin, pausing near the door. "For what?"

"Two years ago, when we met, I blew you off, and it was rude of me," she said in a frank tone that held self-recrimination.

Stunned by her words, he struggled to respond. He'd figured she hadn't remembered him. Apparently, she had. "I wouldn't say you were rude," he finally said. "More like uninterested." He shrugged. "That's okay."

She bit her lip, drawing his eyes to her mouth. His heart slammed against his ribs. She was so pretty. Vulnerable. In need of protection. From him even.

"The problem was…" she said in a soft voice that wrapped around him and held on. "I was interested."

His pulse surged. Really? She'd been interested? "That was a problem?"

A faint smile touched her lips. "Yes. For many reasons."

Not sure whether to be insulted or thrilled, he leaned against the doorjamb and crossed his arms at his chest. "Care to share?"

"Not particularly."

Her honesty had him wanting to stride across the room and kiss her. He locked eyes with her. "I'm not sure what I'm supposed to do with this information." Did this mean she was interested now? His heart hammered a staccato tempo and made his blood dance. If she were interested, what would he do about it?

Nothing.

He couldn't.

He wouldn't.

"You're risking your life for me," she stated. "I just thought you should know."

He steeled himself against the affection taking root. "I'm doing my job."

He couldn't let himself become emotionally involved. He really wanted to think there was nothing personal about protecting the judge. But now that she'd admitted she had been interested in him and for some reason known only to her had shut him down, he couldn't stop the yearning to know just how interested she'd been. And if she still was. Because he was certainly interested in her.

Swallowing back the admission, he said, "I'll let you settle in. Breakfast will be ready in an hour."

He backed out of the room, shutting the door softly behind him. Running a hand down his bristled face, he took a deep breath. He really needed to keep his perspective. In the grand scheme of things, it didn't matter. Protecting her was what mattered. She was under his protection, and he had an obligation to keep things between them professional. He needed to keep a clear head. Becoming emotionally involved with Adele would be a complication neither of them needed.

With that thought firmly in place, Brian freshened up in his own en suite and then headed for the kitchen.

Conlan was sitting at the counter with his phone to his ear. He looked up when Brian approached. "Yeah, I'll let him know. Talk to you soon." He disconnected the call.

Brian arched an eyebrow.

"That was Jace," Conlan told him. "He said to let you know that they can't find anything linking Teresa Watts to the gas heater left in the crawl space of the house. They're checking into the judge's house cleaning service. But so far they've come up empty."

As frustrating as that news was, Brian was glad that Adele's dog sitter wasn't in league with the bad guys.

Scout trotted over and nudged him with his nose. "I'm going to take the dog out."

Brian opened the sliding-glass door, allowing Scout to dart out to the large patch of grass at the end of the deck steps. Keeping an eye on Scout, Brian breathed in the fresh air. It smelled different here in the Hill Country than it did in the city. As a kid, he'd always loved coming to the lake.

Scout's nose went to the ground and followed a scent to the tall-grass-covered berm between the house and the lakeshore. For a moment, Brian lost sight of the dog. Then he caught sight of the black-and-white spots moving through the grass. Brian gave a whistle and Scout came running back. "Good boy. Let's get you a treat."

Back inside, Brian shut just the screen door on the slider, letting in the fresh morning air. Then he went to the pantry and rummaged through a box of treats reserved for his cousin Danny's Great Dane. Because the treats were so big, he broke one in two and gave it to Scout, setting the other half on the kitchen counter. He unloaded the groceries they'd brought, setting out everything for the breakfast he'd promised Adele.

"What can I do to help?" Conlan asked.

"You can do a perimeter check," Brian told the younger deputy. "Take stock. We'll need to set an alarm signal in case we have visitors. There's equipment in my SUV. Three motion-detector trail cameras with WiFi link for the laptop."

Conlan jumped off the stool. "I can take care that." He hustled outside.

Brian hoped they wouldn't need the security measures, but he wasn't about to be caught off guard. Adele was counting on him.

NINE

"Need any help?"

Brian's gaze was riveted by Adele as she came down the staircase. She'd put her hair up into a ponytail, revealing the creamy column of her neck. Would her skin be as silky as he imagined?

He averted his eyes from the place where her collarbone peaked out from beneath the sweater she wore and forced himself to focus on the task of cooking. It took a second for his mind to kick into gear.

"You can start toasting and buttering bread," he said, his voice coming out huskier than he'd have liked. "I'll make scrambled eggs with arugula, tomatoes and onion."

"And he's a gourmet chef, too," she quipped as she headed to the loaf of bread sitting out on the counter.

"Toaster's under the cabinet to your left."

"Perfect." They worked in silence as they prepared breakfast. When it was ready and the plates set on the dining table, Brian went to the screen door and gave a shout. "Breakfast."

It didn't take long for Conlan to join them. The three of them ate and their conversation was light, focused on mundane things like books, television shows and movies. He found it interesting that he and Adele shared many of the same tastes, both liking comedies and dramas that touched on serious issues while Conlan, being at least ten years younger, was more into sci-fi and horror.

After they ate and cleaned up their dishes, Adele asked, "Can we take a walk down to the lake?"

Brian looked at her slip-on black shoes. "Did you bring athletic shoes?"

"I did. I'll go change."

Brian watched her run up the stairs. He noticed the younger deputy watching, as well. Jealousy twisted through Brian's gut, unexpected and unwanted. Still, he couldn't keep the bite out of his tone. "Have you set up the alarm system?"

Conlan pivoted, his face flushing guiltily. "There's a lot of access points from the lake. Or on foot, if someone were to park out of view and walk in." His glance moved to Scout, who lay by the screen door, his head up and ears alert, no doubt hearing the squawks of the wrens who called the lake area home. "It was good thinking to bring a canine along."

"He's a good boy and will sound an alarm if anyone gets close to the house."

"I marked spots for the motion detectors for the front porch and the back, but I need some tools. Also, I was thinking it might be good to do a wider perimeter. Any chance you have any empty soda cans we could string up between the trees?"

Brian nodded, liking the idea. "Old school. Good thinking. I'm sure there are some in the recycle bins in the garage, along with any tools you'll require."

Conlan looked pleased at Brian's praise. "Shouldn't take me too long to set it all up."

"We'll be down at the lake if you need us."

Adele jogged down the staircase. Not only had she changed out of her dress shoes, but she had exchanged her black slacks and sweater for jeans and a zip-up hoodie in the purple and yellow colors of a popular Texas university.

With her auburn hair swept up into a high ponytail, the whole look made her appear years younger than the thirty-six years he knew her to be. Not trusting himself to comment for fear he'd make a fool of himself, he turned on his heel and headed to the slider. He opened the screen door, letting Scout bolt through before he stepped onto the cedar-plank deck.

He could feel Adele behind him even before she said, "Do you think I should put him on a leash?"

"He'll come to a whistle. I don't think he'll wander far."

Brian headed down the deck steps with Adele hot on his heels. They had to go single file along the trail leading through the tall-grassed berm that dropped down onto the sandy shoreline. Brian went first, hopping onto the sand and turning to reach out his hand. Adele grinned at him, took his hand and then jumped, landing on both feet and kicking up some sand. His heart contracted with affection, liking how being here had eased her tension. She appeared calmer and he was glad he'd brought her here.

She breathed in deep. "I already feel like a weight has been lifted."

"Don't get too comfortable," he couldn't refrain from warning, though he hated to dim her enjoyment. "When we drop our guard is when we are most vulnerable."

She gave him a hooded glance that lingered and made him wonder what she was thinking. Was she finding it as hard to keep the attraction arcing between them in check as he was?

"Truth," she replied.

He had his suspicion she wasn't only referring to the danger but to something else. Something personal, which brought him back to their earlier conversation.

Unable to contain the need to know, he asked, "Are you going to tell me why you brushed me off two years ago?"

She walked away from him. "Maybe I didn't believe a guy like you could really be interested in me."

"Not buying the excuse," he called after her.

The sun was now over the lake and more people were out enjoying the mild February weather. His gaze scanned each boat, noting the call numbers and filing them away. Nothing looked out of the ordinary. If somebody wasn't threatening the judge's life, this would be a glorious morning with a beautiful woman. A woman who was trying not to let on that she was attracted to him. His ego puffed up and he quickly put a pin in it. But his curiosity wasn't as easily dissuaded. He caught up to Adele. "Why aren't you married?"

Her steps faltered. "That's a very impertinent question."

He grinned. "I'm an impertinent guy."

She slanted him a quick glance. "No, you're not. You strike me as a very controlled person who very rarely acts impulsively." She waved a delicate hand at him. "Despite how you try to come across."

He barked out a laugh. "And how do I come across?"

"Laid-back surfer dude. A ladies' man some of the time. And good ole cowboy the rest of the time. But in the last few days, I've seen a side of you I doubt you show often. You have hidden depths. You can be serious and very detail-oriented. You think through every move you make and plan for all contingencies."

Had she been studying him? He wasn't sure how he felt about her assessment. Especially since it rang true. He did like to present the world with one of his two personas; it kept people, mostly the bad guys, guessing. "Being a bit of a chameleon helps me do my job. Let's people underestimate me."

"Good information to know. I won't underestimate you." She looked down the beach, shielding her eyes from the sun. "Race you to that piece of driftwood."

He scoffed silently. She was really good at deflecting. He let her. "You're on."

"Go!" She took off, her feet kicking up sand behind her. Scout bound up to her, jumping with excitement to see his mistress running.

Brian laughed and ran after her. "Not fair."

After spending most of the morning on the lakeshore, taking turns with Brian throwing pieces of driftwood into the water for Scout to retrieve, Adele couldn't believe how much she was coming to care for the handsome marshal. He was so patient with Scout's constant attention and with her own reticence to talk. He seemed to understand her need to back away from the painful personal conversations that dredged up the longing to tell him about her past.

"Let's head back," Brian said. "I could use some water and I'm sure this one could, too." He knelt to scrub Scout behind the ears.

Tender affection filled Adele. The man was so thoughtful and considerate. She doubted those traits were inherent with the job, as was his courage and dedication.

They walked back toward the house. When they reached the edge of the berm, Brian scrambled up first. Standing on the edge of the berm, he held out his hands to her. She could've easily followed in his footsteps, climbing up as he had, but she took the opportunity to place both her hands in his, the rough texture of his palms scraping across her own with heated friction.

Stifling the flaring attraction, she let him pull her up the berm to stand on the edge with him, her feet planted between his larger ones.

For a heartbeat, they stood there frozen in place, his hands keeping her anchored to him. She met his beautiful eyes. His hooded gaze dropped to her lips and she wondered, Would he kiss her?

Did she want him to?

Her heart rate doubled, and she swayed toward him as the answer to the question burned bright in her mind. Yes. Please.

His lips parted on a silent exhale and he stepped back, dispelling the moment. Disappointment rippled through her like water down a drain spout. What was wrong with her? She knew better than to let down her guard and give in to feelings of affection and attraction.

This man was here only because he'd been assigned to protect her, not because he wanted to be with her. But the knowledge did nothing to alleviate the yearnings taking root inside her heart. Was she fabricating feelings because she felt safe?

He tugged her forward, away from the edge, both physically and metaphorically. She almost laughed.

Tightening his hold of her hand when she tried to let him go, they made their way through the tall grass. Deciding not to make an issue of the contact, she kept pace while Scout ran and jumped through the grass, appearing and disappearing until he made it to the pristine lawn of the backyard where he waited for them. There was no denying the smile on Scout's black-and-white face. The dog was happy. Adele was happy, too. She only wished this feeling was for real and sustainable. But it wasn't, couldn't be, and he deserved to know why.

Brian halted abruptly. She bumped into him, feeling the rigid tension in his body. A jolt of panic sent her heart thumping against her ribs. She clutched his arm. He crouched down and she followed suit. Were they ducking out of sight of a sniper's rifle scope?

She kept her head low. But then she noticed Brian reaching forward along the edge of the path and touching a nearly invisible line of fishing wire. He gave it a little tug. The sound of clanging cans assaulted their ears.

Brian grinned at her. "A makeshift alarm. Scout was smart enough to jump over it. Hopefully, anyone trying to sneak up to the house wouldn't be as intelligent as your dog."

She barked out a relieved laugh. "Joe Conlan, I take it."

Brian tugged her to her feet and, retaining her hand, gingerly stepped over the wire. She followed suit.

"Can we walk around to the front porch?" she asked, not yet ready to go inside.

Surprise flared in Brian's eyes, but he nodded. When they reached the front of the house, she stopped, squeezing his hand. The need to confide in him had her heart thumping and her pulse skittering, but the anxiety she normally battled didn't rise. The urge to talk was profoundly different. Rather than fight it, she asked, "Can we take a seat?"

Gesturing for her to take the nearest rocking chair, he stepped past her and sat in the other one. With the toe of her foot, she sent the chair rocking. It was so peaceful here and she hated to bring up something unpleasant. But he needed to know. "You asked me earlier why I've never married."

Brian stared at her intently. "I did. And you deflected."

She shrugged. "A defense mechanism."

"I get it. I do the same."

His admission warmed her. They were alike in many ways. "Why aren't you married?"

One side of his mouth lifted. "I thought this discussion was going to be about you?"

She laughed, liking him. "Nice deflection."

He grinned.

Her heart tumbled.

He reached for her hand again, closing his fingers around hers. She didn't feel in the least bit anxious or the need to jerk away from his touch. Strange. Yet, she couldn't say his touch was unwanted. It was nice to have an anchor. Especially for what she needed to tell him.

Where to begin? With her foolish notions of romance when she was teen? Or the easiness to be fooled by a handsome face and nice manners? She decided to just jump in. "You know about the assault from college."

He ran his thumb along hers. "Just what you have told me."

She turned to look at him, surprised. "I would've thought you read up on me, especially after I'd mentioned it before."

"Normally, I would have. But everything happened so quickly in the beginning. Being assigned to your protection detail, getting you to your house from the hospital, then from the house to here, hasn't left a lot of time for me to do any sort of background work."

She couldn't keep the astonishment from her tone. "Not even two years ago?"

"I didn't realize you were the judge being honored at the gala until you walked out on stage to give your speech." His look was soft, alluring. She could feel herself leaning toward him. "Then it made total sense why you would turn down my invitation to dinner. You were—are—completely out of my league."

She frowned at that assessment. "Don't sell yourself short. It's unbecoming."

He arched an eyebrow. "Duly noted."

Her conscience poked at her. She had to be honest with him, explain her past so that he could understand. "My being a judge had nothing to do with why I turned you down."

Silence ensued between them, though it wasn't necessarily awkward or tense. *Companionable* was the word that came to mind. He was giving her time, which only made him more endearing.

Overhead, a bird screeched as it flew across the sky, a dark shape against the blue, then it made a sharp descent to the lake, grabbing up some unsuspecting fish before ascending into the sky and flying away. How many times had she wished she could just fly away and never have to face reality?

Too often. But she realized she didn't want to right now. Not with Brian here at her side. For some reason, he gave her strength and determination she'd never expected.

"The assault happened my freshman year," she said, her voice hushed as if somehow speaking softly wouldn't disturb the past. "My first semester and my first time away from home. The first time I'd had male attention that my parents hadn't vetted. His name was Richard Overstreet. He was flattering, charming even. I'd never had anyone be so..." She couldn't find the word for such focused attention. "Now I understand Richard's obsessive nature, but back then, I didn't."

A visible shudder wracked over Brian. "He was stalking you?"

"I don't know that you can classify his actions as 'stalking' when I welcomed the attention." Shame flooded her. She'd been so naïve. So eager to be wanted, she hadn't seen the warning signs at first. "You see, I grew up with all the same kids from elementary school to high school. The guys were more like brothers. So Richard's devotion was new and exciting. But his obsession with me became too much. Scary. I broke it off with him. He didn't take it well."

Brian squeezed her hand but didn't say anything. She was grateful that he was letting her tell the story her way, without interruption.

"A week after we broke up, I was coming out of the library. I always took the back door because it was closest to my dorm. He was waiting for me." She could still see him standing there in the shadows, his shoulders hunched, his hands jammed into his pockets. So misleading. "He appeared heartbroken at first, saying he wanted me back." She took a shuddering breath. "I said no. He became agitated, saying cruel things, and then he grabbed me, moving so fast I didn't have time to react. He dragged me into the bushes. I screamed and fought." The memory was a horrible nightmare. "A campus security guard heard me and came running. A small blessing."

She tightened her hold on Brian's hand and forced the words out. "The security guard and Richard fought. The guard tried to subdue him, but Richard was much stronger than people gave him credit for. He was slender, but he worked out regularly. Richard pushed the guard down then jumped on him, slamming his head into the concrete walkway. He died."

She remembered the blood and the fear. The rage.

"But Richard didn't get away?"

Brian's softly asked question drew her eyes to his. "No, he didn't. Other people heard my screams and heard Richard and the guard fighting. Two of the campus football team members grabbed Richard and held him until the police came. Richard was arrested, tried and convicted of murder."

"I'm sorry that happened to you. I'm sorry the security guard died. It shouldn't have happened." Brian tucked a stray strand of hair behind her ear, his touch soft and lingering. "Is Richard the reason you've never married?"

She sighed, desperately trying to tamp down the white-hot anxiety rearing its ugly head. She wanted to lean into his touch, to have him hold her and tell her everything would be all right. But would doing so help alleviate her worries? Or only create new ones? As safe as she felt with Brian, she had to guard her heart. She sat straighter and said for both of their benefit, "Obviously my judgment where men are concerned is not good."

Though for some reason she had a hard time

believing Brian was anything other than how he appeared to her. Steadfast, honorable and caring. Unfortunately, she knew firsthand the deception a handsome face and good manners could hide.

"The reason I'm telling you this is that Richard's parole hearing is in four days. I need to appear, and make sure he doesn't get out."

For a beat, Brian's handsome face held a stunned expression then his eyebrows lowered. "This changes things."

Her breathing stilled. "How so?"

"I'm not sure, yet. But it might be motive for somebody wanting you dead. Someone doesn't want you to go to that hearing."

Her stomach knotted. She hadn't made the possible connection. Could it be true? Was someone trying to stop her from testifying? But who?

The next day, Brian paced the living room waiting for Adele to come down. He'd heard her in the kitchen while he'd been on the phone with Sera and Jace, tracking down information on Richard Overstreet, the man who had assaulted Adele when she was in college.

Yesterday, as he'd listened to her telling him about her past, it had taken all his willpower not to fold her into his arms and promise she'd never suffer like that again. It hurt to think she blamed herself for the horrible actions of someone else. He didn't know how to help her or even if it was his place to do so. But, God willing, he could discover if the danger threatening her life came from her past.

"Good morning." Adele descended the stairs wearing black jeans and an emerald-green, long-sleeved shirt. It was a fabulous choice for her. The morning sunlight streaming through the floor-to-ceiling windows sparkled on her fiery hair. She'd clipped back the sides of her hair, letting the ends rest against her shoulders.

"Morning." His voice came out husky and low. He cleared his throat. "I have an address."

She cocked her head. "For?"

He gave her a sheepish grin. His mouth was moving faster than his brain. "Sorry. It turns out Richard Overstreet's mother lives in Austin, and Sera found a Trevor Overstreet in the DMV records," Brian said. "We'll visit her and see if she can give us any useful information."

"You can't honestly believe after all this time Richard's family is coming after me? Why would they do that?"

"Because you're the only obstacle standing in the way of him gaining parole."

TEN

Brian geared up, putting on a flak vest beneath his US marshals' jacket. He handed Adele the extra flak vest he'd grabbed from the back compartment of the SUV. It was a smaller one, which Sera usually wore, and it would fit Adele. "Put this on and cover it with a sweater or jacket."

She stared at the dark gray vest with the US marshals' logo in bright yellow across the front and back. "Should we be going if you're expecting trouble?"

"I always expect trouble, even when the likelihood is slim," he informed her. "Sera's off chasing down a lead on Maria Montoya." At Adele's questioning look he said, "Tomas Garcia's illegitimate daughter, suspected of claiming her father's role as head of the Garcia cartel."

Pulling a face, Adele said, "That doesn't

sound good. I thought the cartel was dismantled when Tomas was arrested."

"What's that saying, cut off the head and another grows back? But I'm sure Sera will succeed in finding Maria. She's determined. And Jace has been called to another case. If we don't go now and figure this out, we will be in hiding for a long time waiting for somebody else to do it. This is only a fact-finding mission. A simple conversation with Mrs. Overstreet."

"I doubt it will be simple for her, having the woman who put her son in jail at her door."

"You'll stay in the car."

She gave him a look rife with meaning that he didn't understand. Then she took the flak vest and slipped it on over her long-sleeved shirt. "What about Scout?"

"We bring him and Joe with us."

Adele nodded. "I'll put on a jacket to cover this and be right back."

Brian went outside to find Joe and Scout walking the perimeter. He filled Joe in on the situation.

"Give me a minute to grab my gear," Joe said. He took off for the house, leaving Scout with Brian.

Staring out at the water dappled in morning sunlight, Brian felt Scout lean against his legs. "Between you and me," Brian said, "this might be a wild-goose chase. But it beats sitting around here twiddling our thumbs."

Usually, Brian preferred actively tracking fugitives over witness protection. But the judge was his responsibility. Ending this nightmare for her by pursuing the possibility that someone in Overstreet's family was out to get Adele was the best way to protect her. "Okay, boy, let's get you leashed up."

The drive to Austin was uneventful. Brian kept an eye on the rear-view mirror just in case of a tail, but he saw nothing to suggest they were being followed. He shifted his gaze and met Adele's. She sat in the back on the passenger's-side bench seat, Scout laying across her lap. The dog was tethered to the seat buckle. She smiled at Brian, and his heart gave a bump. He returned his attention to the road.

"Turn right up ahead," Joe said, navigating from the front passenger seat and reading the directions Sera had sent to the Overstreet household.

"I'm going to park a few houses away," Brian said. "I will approach the house. You and Scout keep watch."

"I've got your back," Joe said as Brian pulled the SUV to the curb.

Adele jumped out of the vehicle. "I'm coming with you."

"That's a negative," he said. "You hang back here."

"Not happening." She walked away from him, toward the house.

His stomach knotted. He should have known the stubborn woman wouldn't do as told. He had to admit he admired her nerve. Approaching the mother of the man who'd assaulted her would be difficult. Who knew what kind of reaction Mrs. Overstreet would have? It would be up to Brian to provide a barrier to the judge.

Scout barked a protest at being left behind. Brian contemplated bringing Scout but thought that might complicate matters if the family had an aversion to dogs.

"Let me do the talking," he told Adele as he caught up to her and opened the gate to the small fenced yard.

He put a hand at her elbow once they were both in the yard and paused, letting his senses acclimate. Head on a swivel, he took in the neighbors' homes on both sides of the Overstreet house and across the street. Not seeing anyone staring back, he then focused his gaze on the A-frame at the end of the short concrete walkway.

The house wasn't large by most standards and was in need of some repairs. Paint curled from the siding, the stairs to the porch sagged slightly to one side. He studied the windows. No movement behind the curtains. Tucking Adele behind him, he stepped onto the porch, the boards creaking beneath his weight. He tried the silver doorbell but heard no sound from within. He banged his knuckles hard against the doorjamb.

From somewhere on the other side of the door, he heard movement. A few seconds later, the door creaked open, and a woman wearing a housecoat and a bandanna around her head stared out at them. She had sunken cheeks and big, luminous, dark eyes rimmed red. He noticed an IV attached to her hand and mobile IV pole next to her.

"What you want?" the woman practically growled.

"Are you Mrs. Irene Overstreet?" Brian asked, peering over her shoulder to see if anyone else was inside.

"Who's asking?" she rasped.

"Deputy US marshal Brian Forrester." Brian showed her his badge.

The woman's eyes widened then narrowed as she glared past Brian. She lifted a bony finger and pointed it at Adele. "You."

The amount of accusation in her tone raised the fine hairs on Brian's neck. "May we come in?"

Confusion joined the hostility in her eyes. "Why?"

Adele stepped forward. "We're sorry to bother you, Mrs. Overstreet. We just have some questions. Obviously, you know who I am. Please. It's important."

"Why are you here?" Irene asked, her voice laced with antagonism. "Haven't you done enough to ruin my life?"

Brian heard Adele's sharp intake of breath. But she straightened her shoulders and lifted her chin. "I need to talk to you about Richard's case."

For a long moment, Irene Overstreet stared at them before she stepped aside, widening the door. Brian held Adele back so that he could go through first and assess the situation. She closed the front door with a soft click. The house was shrouded in shadow, with all the curtains pulled closed. Light from a flickering TV illuminated a recliner and a small end table filled with pill bottles.

Irene shuffled away from the door and into the living area, slowly lowering herself into the recliner. Off to one side of the recliner was a short two-person couch. She waved a hand. "Sit. I don't like craning my neck to see you."

Brian nudged Adele to the couch, where she sat. He remained standing off to the side where he had a good view of the front door, the kitchen, and down the hallway. All access points that needed to be watched.

"What do you want?" Irene's voice shook, as if the effort to get up and answer the door had taken all of her energy.

"I'm sorry to see that you are ill," Adele said, her voice filled with compassion.

"Save it. You put my boy in prison. You don't care about me or my family."

Adele scooted to the edge of the couch. Her hands rested on her knees, her knuckles whitening as she tightened her grip. "I do care. What your son did to me, did to the campus security guard, was wrong. He had to pay the price for his actions."

"It's been fifteen years. It's time you let him out." Irene's eyes filled with tears. "As you can see, I am ill. I don't have much longer. I want my son home."

Though Brian held pity for the woman, they weren't here to discuss the man in jail. "You have another son. Where is he?"

"How should I know? It's classified." Irene sneered at him.

"Classified?" Adele glanced up at Brian then back to Irene. "What do you mean?"

"He's military. I don't hear from him often. And when I do, he can't tell me where he's at." She eyed them both suspiciously. "Are you trying to test me? What is this about?"

"What branch of the military is he in?" Brian asked.

"Army."

After digesting this new information, Brian decided it was time to go. They wouldn't get more out Irene Overstreet. "Thank you for your time." Brian held out a hand for Adele. She slipped her hand into his and let him pull her to her feet.

"Do you have help?" Adele asked Irene.

Her lips twisted. "My neighbor checks in on me. Not that it's any of your business."

Adele took two steps then stopped. Her hand reached for a photo of three young boys sitting on the mantel over the fireplace. She showed it to Brian and pointed a finger to the older of the boys. "Richard."

His eyebrows rose. Richard and his brothers, who were clearly twins.

Brian held the photo out so Irene could view

it. "Richard is in prison. Your son, Trevor is in the army. Where's the other one?"

Irene's shoulders hunched and her chin dropped. "Gone." When she lifted her gaze, malice lightened the dark depths. "He ran away when he was fifteen."

"You have no idea where he is?" Brian pressed.

"Dead."

"I'm so sorry for your loss. What are their names?" Adele asked gently.

"Travis and Trevor." She glared at Adele. "Save your pity. If you feel bad, then release my son."

"That's not possible," Adele said.

Irene's lips stretched in a gruesome semblance of a smile. Her cheekbones protruded and her lips thinned. "Anything is possible."

Uneasy with the situation, Brian set the photo back on the mantel. Then he tugged Adele out of the oppressive house, closing the door softly behind him.

As soon as they were out on the sidewalk, he grabbed his phone and called the tech support at the marshals' headquarters.

Penelope Lane answered on the first ring. "What can I do for you, Deputy Forrester?"

The no-nonsense tech expert wasn't much

for pleasantries. "I need you to find everything you can on a Travis Overstreet and a Trevor Overstreet."

"On it," Penny said. "I'm surprised you're not having Sera do this since she likes to pretend to be the tech guru of your group."

Sera didn't pretend. She was good with the computer. But she was better out in the field. It was well known in the office that the two women were at odds with each other but kept it a friendly rivalry. "Best not let Sera hear such words," he teased.

"I know, I know," Penelope said. "I just don't want to get into a turf war with Deputy Morales. I'll text you everything I find."

"I appreciate it," Brian told her and hung up.

When he and Adele reached the SUV, he realized that Joe and Scout were nowhere in sight. Apprehension twisted Brian's gut.

"Where are they?" Adele asked, her voice filled with anxiety.

Then Scout and Joe appeared from around the corner of the Overstreet house. They hurried to the vehicle.

"Dog had to do his business," Joe told them. "Figured we could do a little recon around the back. Place has seen better days."

Relieved to see the pair, Brian nodded and

opened the rear passenger door for Adele and Scout. Once they were situated, he went around to the driver's side. Joe resumed his place in the front passenger seat.

Brian put the key in the ignition and turned as he said, "We learned—"

The engine made a sputtering noise and every alarm bell in Brian's system went on alert.

He turned the engine off. "Everyone out now."

Quickly, he climbed out and opened the back door for Adele and Scout. He moved them far from the vehicle.

Joe joined them on the opposite side of the street. "What's going on? Do you think someone tampered with the vehicle?"

"Only one way to know." Brian approached the vehicle cautiously, stopping a few feet away. He bent down to look underneath the chassis. He saw a rudimentary bundle of C-4 sticks and wires plugged into the starter.

It was remarkable the device hadn't gone off. If he had tried the engine one more time, the vehicle would've exploded.

Adele wrapped her arms around her middle, Scout's leash held tight in one hand. Anxiety threatened to overwhelm her. The quiet, suburban street on the outskirts of Austin, Texas, was a buzz of activity. Much different than when she, Brian and Joe had arrived earlier.

Agents from both the FBI and ATF had arrived, along with the Austin PD bomb squad. More US marshals had also descended, creating a barrier around Adele, as if she wasn't spectacle enough for the neighbors now gathering in their yards or peering out their windows, as Mrs. Overstreet was doing now. What was the woman thinking? Adele felt bad for the ill widow, but that sympathy wasn't enough to thwart Adele from testifying at her son's upcoming parole hearing.

Tension ratcheted through her muscles, along her spine and shoulders, as she watched the bomb technicians remove the explosive device from underneath the SUV. Beside her, Brian shifted his stance, clearly eager to talk to the bomb squad. But he remained steadily at her side, which she appreciated. An FBI agent approached with irritation etched on his face. Directed at her and Brian? Or at the bomber?

"Judge Weston, I'm special agent Darius Vargas with the FBI. I'd like to ask you some questions. Alone."

"Not leaving her side," Brian stated firmly.

Vargas held Brian's stare. "Fine. But know I'll be speaking with your boss."

The words sounded ominously like a threat. Adele hated to think Brian would catch heat from his boss.

Turning his focus to Adele, Vargas prompted, "Explain to me exactly why you are here."

Adele glanced at Brian. "We—"

"We've been looking into Judge Weston's old cases, trying to determine who might be targeting her," Brian said.

Vargas's eyes narrowed on Brian. "And you decided to visit the mother of the man she put in prison before she became a judge?"

Adele grimaced. Obviously, the FBI knew about Richard and the assault in college. "This was merely an information-gathering visit." She hadn't really thought they'd find answers here. "I was safe with Bri—Deputy Forrester and Deputy Conlan."

Vargas's gaze snapped to her. "Information gathering is my job. You should have reached out and we would've done the legwork." His gaze bounced back to Brian. "You know better."

"My apologies."

Brian looked anything but apologetic. No doubt to him this was a case of begging forgiveness rather than asking for permission. A flutter of guilt beneath Adele's breastbone had her blurting out, "This is my fault."

Vargas's steely-eyed stare once again skewered her to the spot. "You should've known better, as well, Your Honor. Coming out of hiding put you in danger."

"I took evasive measures," Brian said. "We were not tailed here."

"Obviously, you were, or your vehicle wouldn't have been rigged to explode," the agent said. "What did you learn from Mrs. Overstreet?"

"She's gravely ill," Adele told the agent. "She had three sons. One of whom apparently died a long time ago. And the other is serving in the military. Army."

"I'll establish the whereabouts of the soldier," Vargas said.

Conlan stepped up at that moment. Vargas turned his attention onto the marshal. "Explain to me how someone got that close to the SUV."

Joe looked sheepish. "The dog had to go. I thought I'd walk around the back of the house. There are two more entry points. There's a car in the garage under a tarp."

"How long were you gone?"

"Two minutes, max."

"Somebody was waiting for an opportunity," Vargas stated. "If you weren't followed, then how would the perpetrator know you would be here?"

"I don't have an answer," Brian said, and the grim tone of his voice sent a shiver over Adele. She shuddered at the creepy notion that whomever had sabotaged the SUV was somehow keeping tabs on her. But how?

"I'll have agents take you back to your safe house," Vargas said. "Do not leave again without a full escort."

Brian nodded and put his hand to the small of Adele's back, creating a warm spot that rippled over her skin. "Count on it."

They all climbed into an FBI SUV. Scout sat on the back seat, between Brian and Adele. Another set of FBI agents followed with Joe on the drive back to San Antonio where they all transferred to another SUV driven by Marshal Gavin Armstrong.

When they arrived at the lake house, Scout took off for the backside of the yard and Joe went after him.

Brian touched Adele's elbow. "You go on in."

No doubt he was going to be read the riot act by his boss.

She turned to Gavin. "Marshal, this isn't Brian's fault."

"Adele." Brian's tone held a warning. Apparently, he didn't want her coming to his defense. Well, too bad.

"I appreciate what you're trying to do, Judge Weston," Gavin said, "but Deputy Forrester broke protocol. There will be consequences."

"He only just learned today that I'm scheduled to testify at Richard Overstreet's parole hearing in three days." She glanced at Brian, meeting his scowl. "I don't think either of us really believed Richard's family had anything to do with the attempts on my life."

"We couldn't rule it out, either," Brian stated. To his boss, he said, "I take full responsibility for breaking protocol."

"This isn't like you, Brian," Gavin said. "Do not let it happen again."

Properly contrite, Brian said, "I won't, sir."

"As soon as Jace is done with his current assignment, I will have him come out and relieve Joe."

"This isn't Joe's—" Adele said at the same time as Brian said, "It's not Conlan's—"

Adele could barely suppress her smile at how she and Brian both came to Joe's defense.

Gavin held up a hand. "Doesn't matter. I

need someone with more experience and who won't let you do anything out of bounds."

"Yes, sir."

Gavin gave a sharp nod then turned on his heels and headed back to his SUV. Joe and Scout came around from the back of the house.

"How much trouble are we in?" Joe asked.

"Some," Brian said. "This won't fall back on you."

Adele didn't like the thought that Brian's career could be impacted because of her. If she could set him free, she would, but she needed him here to protect her. To keep her safe in hiding. Because she trusted him. Cared for him, too. But that shouldn't be a part of the equation.

Once inside the house, Adele and Scout headed upstairs. Needing to hear her mother's voice, she dialed her parents' home phone.

Her mom answered on the third ring. "Hello, dear."

"Hi, Mom."

"Are you okay?" her mother asked.

A loaded question. "If I say fine, will you believe me?"

"No. What's going on?"

Loath to worry her mother any more than she already was, Adele said, "I'm going stir crazy. We haven't narrowed down who might be after me. It's like looking for the proverbial needle in the haystack. Or rather, file folders."

"I can appreciate how anxious you must be, but I am glad you are there with Deputy Forrester. Your father asked around about him and heard good things. We like him."

"I do, too, Mom," Adele confessed.

"Like as in *like*?" There was no doubting the hopeful tone in her mother's voice.

Adele sighed. "It doesn't matter which. I'm nothing more than a job to him. When this is over, we will go our separate ways." The thought didn't sit well. What if she wanted more from him? Would he want more from her? Did she dare believe there could be more?

"You don't have to go your separate ways," her mother insisted. "You both live and work in San Antonio."

Adele winced at how closely her mother's words mirrored her thoughts. "That's not the problem, Mom, and you know it."

Her mother's sigh, so like her own, reverberated in Adele's ear. "You can't let one horrible incident in your life taint your future. You've done enough of that already. It's been fifteen years. If you don't risk your heart, you will never know what's possible."

Adele closed her eyes and pinched the bridge

of her nose. They'd had this discussion numerous times. Only this time, for some reason, her mother's words seemed to dig in and take root. But she couldn't think that way. Not now. She needed to stay detached, unemotional, so she and Brian could work together and find out who wanted her dead and not have emotions cloud the situation. Easier said than done. "Thanks for the pep talk, Mom. I appreciate you. Give my love to Dad."

"Of course, dear. We love you and are praying for you."

"I appreciate your prayers."

Adele hung up and said a prayer of her own, asking God to bring clarity and closure to the situation. What had she done that was so bad to make someone want her dead?

ELEVEN

Adele went back downstairs and found Brian organizing the file folders and the boxes. He looked up as she approached. "I figure we should get back to this. I sent Penelope a list of names to check the whereabouts on."

"Penelope?" Adele took a seat on the couch and picked up the top file folder on the coffee table. "You mentioned her before."

"She's the computer tech person for our office."

"I thought Sera did a lot of the tech work?"

"She does. She's good at it. But she's a better field agent. And that's where her interests lie."

"It's nice to have a team of experts at my disposal," Adele said. She didn't know what she would do if she had to face all of this alone. But the protection from the US marshals came with the job. She'd never thought she'd need it, but was thankful for it.

They worked for several hours, going through

more boxes of case files. Walking down these particular memory lanes wasn't exactly a fun trip. As a prosecutor, she'd tried a variety of cases ranging from domestic abuse, grand theft, embezzlement to murder. As a judge, she'd presided over many similar cases. It was depressing to view her career in such harsh reality. As the day waned toward nightfall, they'd come up with another list of names for Penelope to locate.

Brian's cell phone trilled from his pocket. He glanced at the caller ID then pushed the button. "Hi, Sera, I'm putting you on speakerphone. Adele is with me."

"Hold on to your hats, people." Sera's voice held a strange tone that sent a shiver down Adele's spine. She exchanged a grim, concerned glance with Brian.

"What gives?" Brian asked.

"Dude, the DOJ's servers have been hacked."

Adele's stomach dropped. "That could compromise a lot of DOJ cases."

"That is the prevailing thought," Sera replied. "However, I've been working with Penelope and the DOJ and we discovered that the only files that were accessed were the personnel files for Brian."

Shock gripped Adele in a tight vice, closing her throat.

"How deep did they go?" The razor-sharp tone of Brian's voice ratcheted up Adele's building panic.

"Very deep," Sera said. "They looked into everyone in your family, including your grandparents."

"That means our location has been compromised."

Adele grabbed Brian's arm. "What do we do?"

"We get out of here."

Brian's heart thumped in his chest, and his pulse pounded in his ears. Adele's would-be assassin no doubt knew about the lake house. He had to get her out now. "Go pack your bag, quick."

Adele didn't waste any time. She scrambled off the couch and ran up the stairs. Scout chased after her, barking as if to ask what had her so upset.

Brian picked up the phone and took it off speaker. "How much time do we have?"

"Not long. The breach happened about two hours ago. It took me a while to get past the virus they'd uploaded to see what they had accessed."

Brian rubbed the back of his neck then he was moving across the room to warn Joe. "Send a team to meet us. We'll leave in five."

He hung up and then banged on the door to the room Joe occupied.

It swung open and the deputy blinked at Brian. "Trouble?"

"Yes. Our location has been compromised. We leave in five."

Without a word, Conlan turned, throwing his things back into his go-bag. Brian returned to the living room, grabbed Scout's leash and dog food. He didn't need his things. He could come back to get them later. He checked his weapon, then tucked it into the holster at his waist. Adele returned with only her purse slung over her shoulder and Scout at her side.

"I can get everything when we're safe," she said. "Let's go."

Pleased by her attitude, Brian handed her Scout's leash then headed for the front door.

"Brian," Adele said, indicating Scout, who had moved to the sliding window, staring out at the night. The dog's ears were back, his tail standing upright. Scout bared his teeth and emitted a low growl.

The clanging of aluminum cans bouncing off each other sent alarm racing down Brian's spine. "Intruders."

The lights went out, throwing the house into shadows despite the moonlight streaming through the windows. Someone had cut the power.

Adele hurried to Brian's side. He gave a short whistle, which brought Scout racing over. Using the flashlight on his phone to light the path, they made their way to the to the front door.

Before they reached it, Conlan stepped out of his room, putting his hand over the light. "We have multiple assailants closing in fast."

Motioning them into the bedroom, Conlan showed Brian the computer screen that was split into two images showing the front and back of the house. An intruder in tactical gear appeared on both screens, each carrying an assault rifle and approaching quickly.

"We go out the side door to the garage." Brian hustled Adele back toward the main living area.

Scout let out a series of frantic barks.

The sound of shattering glass filled the house as a projectile burst through the floor-to-ceiling windows at the back of the house. A hissing sound assaulted the air and smoke filled the living room.

Brian tugged Adele into a crouch and reeled Scout close as they worked their way around to the opposite side of the kitchen island. He grabbed a dishtowel and quickly doused it in water and handed it to her. "Put this over your nose and mouth."

He wished he could do the same for Scout. He grabbed another dishtowel for himself and soaked it in water. Tears from the stinging gas flooded his eyes. He blinked to clear his vision. "The door leading to the garage is on the other side of the pantry."

"This way," Conlan said, moved past them, leading the way.

"Won't we be trapped in the garage?" Adele asked, her voice quaking.

Brian hoped she didn't succumb to a panic attack. But he was prepared to carry her if need be.

"There's another door to the side yard. We'll head down to the dock," Brian told her. "I won't let anything happen to you. Trust me."

"I do trust you." Though her voice still quavered, she sounded adamant. "But you can't make guarantees of something you have no control over."

Her admission of confidence in him touched him deeply. "No, I can't give you guarantees, but I promise I will do everything in my power to keep you safe."

"I believe you."

Adele reached up and grabbed something off the kitchen counter. He wanted to ask what she was doing because the thick smoke made it hard to see what she had in her hand. He had to stay focused. Getting Adele out of the line of fire took precedence.

He hurried her forward and hustled them into the garage where they could inhale untainted air. He closed the door behind him. He tugged Adele along with him as they moved past the bikes lined up, waiting to be ridden, and past the tool bench and then out the side exit.

The cool night brought welcome relief from the fumes of the smoke bomb that had been deployed.

"Brian!"

Adele's warning had Brian pivoting as an assailant came around the side of the garage.

Brian raised his weapon. In the same instant, Adele threw what was in her hand. A knife buried itself in the man's thigh, taking him down.

Stunned and pleased, Brian didn't waste time praising Adele for her quick thinking. Instead, he grabbed her hand and pulled her and Scout toward the grassy berm. He prayed they made it to the boat moored within the boathouse.

"What about Joe?" Adele's heart jammed in her throat.

The other agent had disappeared into the

darkness. She'd heard gunfire. Joe had engaged the gunmen.

"He knows what to do and how to create a diversion to allow us time to get away," Brian said, his voice low. "Backup will be here soon. Joe will stay hidden until they arrive."

Breathing heavy with the exertion, Adele ran alongside Brian through the tall grass toward the lakeshore. She could hear Scout off to her left, keeping pace. Fear dogged her steps. The safe house location had been compromised.

She should have never let Brian bring her back here. She should've gone into hiding in another state or another country, even. Anything to keep this man beside her safe. If he, or Joe, died because of her…another hero's death on her conscience would be more than she could bear.

When they reached the end of the berm, Brian jumped down onto the sandy shore. Moonlight splashed across him as he turned and reached for her. She didn't hesitate, she just jumped straight into his arms. He gathered her close for half a second before setting her on her feet, taking her hand and running for the dock. The wooden slats were slippery beneath her tennis shoes. She could hear the reassuring sound of Scout's nails gripping the wood. They reached the door of the enclosed boathouse at the end of the dock. Brian worked at opening the lock.

Beside her, Scout growled and his tail stood up as he leaned against her leg. Though she couldn't see his eyes, she looked in the direction he faced. Two dark figures burst out from the house and ran toward them. Moonlight and the dark tactical gear they wore made them appear like moving shadows.

One limped badly. She took some satisfaction in knowing she'd slowed them down. But now they were gaining on her, Brian and Scout.

She tapped Brian on the shoulder. "Hurry."

The door swung open and he pulled her through. He gave a whistle and Scout joined them. Brian shut the door, locking it behind them. They were in a dark cavernous space. Adele breathed in the faint smell of gasoline.

Brian moved steadily to the right and, a few seconds later, there was the rumbling noise of a motorized garage door opening, letting in moonlight to reveal a speedboat.

Her blood rushed from her head, making her dizzy. "Brian, there's something you should know."

He unmoored the boat, releasing the knots from their anchors and throwing the dark cables into the bottom of the boat.

"It's going to have to wait," he said.

He stepped sure-footed onto the boat deck. He gave another whistle and Scout jumped in alongside him. Adele stayed rooted where she stood at the edge of the dock.

"No, really. I need to tell you. I don't do water."

"I'm not sure what that means. But we don't have time to dissect it. Give me your hand."

She could see his outstretched arm, his hand reaching for hers, but her muscles were frozen. Fear cascaded through her body like ice water. She didn't know how to swim.

"Adele." Brian's voice held an insistent note.

"I can't."

He stepped back onto the dock and put his arms around her. "Yes, you can. We have to go, now!"

The door they'd just come through rattled as if in exclamation to his pronouncement. He urged her heavy feet forward. Tentatively, she stepped into the boat. The vessel rocked beneath their weight and nausea roiled through her stomach.

Brian led her to a seat. "Tuck your head between your knees."

She did as he suggested. Then the growling of the engine firing up rattled her bones. Scout whined, nudging her with his snout. She wrapped her arms around his neck and held him close while staying below the side of the boat.

From outside the boathouse, she could hear shouts, but the words were indistinguishable over the motor. Then Brian put the boat in Reverse and backed up, moving much faster than she would have expected. Her hands flexed against Scout's body. The front end of the boat grazed the edge of the metal side of the boathouse, the high-pitched noise reverberated down her spine.

Brian turned the wheel and pushed the accelerator, propelling them forward and pushing her back against the seat cushion. The sound of rapid gunfire had Adele squeezing Scout and slipping to the deck. Bullets thumped into the boat. She'd never been so afraid in her life. She prayed fervently for God to see them through this.

More gunfire erupted and the inboard engine sputtered and died. She didn't think this could get any worse as the boat slowly came to a halt, bobbing in the middle of the lake.

Brian grabbed two life vests and helped her to put one on. Then he put a vest on Scout and attached his leash to a hook on the back of the vest.

"What about you?" Adele asked.

"I was a lifeguard as a teen, plus a surfer,

remember," he replied as he lifted Scout over the rim of the boat and set him into the water.

Adele scrambled to her feet. A different kind of terror struck her through the chest. "No. I'm not getting in the water."

"We're sitting ducks out here." There was no mistaking the impatience in his tone.

She heard the crash of water as the men ran into the edge of the lake. More gunfire spit water at them. She screamed and ducked. But the bullets fell short of the boat.

"They can't get us at this distance," Brian assured her. "But eventually they will find a way. We have to swim to the other side of the lake."

She gripped his arm, her nails biting into his flesh. She hoped she didn't draw blood but couldn't seem to let go. "I think I'd rather take my chances in the boat."

He grasped her shoulders and moved her to the edge of the boat. "You'll be okay. I promise."

Gently, he pushed her to a seated position on that very edge of the boat.

"Swing your legs over the side," he instructed.

Shaking with fear, Adele dug deep for her last vestige of courage and pivoted her legs over the edge to dangle into the cold water. Her breath caught. Something nudged her calf and she gasped. Then realized it was Scout.

Gripping the edge of the boat, she slowly allowed Brian to slip her into the water. Her breath came in rapid puffs as her body acclimated to the cool temperature. Then Brian slipped in beside her and pried her fingers from the boat. She bobbed in the water, her hands grasping for Brian. Her mind frantic with fear.

He maneuvered so that he was between her and Scout and faced them.

"Keep your eyes on me," he said.

She did. Focusing on him helped. A little.

Then he proceeded to tow both her and Scout to the shore on the other side.

"Would it help if I kicked?" she asked, hating that she was such a burden.

His grin flashed in the moonlight. "It would. You could even dog paddle."

"Don't make fun," she choked out past the lump of dread in her throat. "I almost drowned as a kid and haven't been able to get back in a pool or any other body of water past my ankles since."

"I didn't know," he said, his voice filled with apology. "I won't let you sink."

"I know you won't." He'd drown first before he let her go under. The knowledge bolstered her courage. She dug deep for her swimming lessons when she was a child. She kicked her legs and fluttered her hands, splashing herself in the face. One of her shoes slipped off. She was terrible at swimming.

"Scoop the water like you're scooping sand," he told her.

She scooped, which worked much better.

Beside her, Scout expertly swam even though she'd never taken him to play in water. By the time they reached the other side of the lake, fatigue weighted her legs and her arms. She crawled onto dry land.

"Looks like the cavalry arrived."

She sat and faced Brian's family's lake house, which was now lit up bright. She could see numerous people in and around the house. She recognized Sera, Jace and Joe. But where were the men chasing them? Had they escaped? Were they, even now, making their way across the lake?

She shivered as questions tormented her mind. "Shouldn't we let them know were here? That we're safe?"

"Not yet."

She didn't know how to do this. Running for her life was as foreign as walking on the moon would be. The muscles at the nape of her neck ached with tension.

Brian unhooked the life vest from around

Scout. Scout gave a mighty shake, sending water flying. Adele fumbled with the clasps on her vest, her hands shaking too hard to squeeze the buckles. He helped her out, his big capable hands steady and sure.

Once free of the vest, she gave a shake similar to Scout's. Hers was more to shake off the fear of drowning and being shot at. Now they had to get to safety. But how?

Terror colored the edges of her sanity. She concentrated on breathing to hold off an attack. This would not be the time to give in to the anxiety gathering steam inside her chest.

Brian grabbed her by the hand, tugging her to the tree line. "We'll use the shadows for cover and work our way around the lake back to the house."

Forcing one wet sock-covered foot in front of her tennis-shoe-covered foot and shivering in her soaked clothes, she followed Brian through the trees with Scout on leash at her side. Fatigue pulled at her limbs. It seemed like an interminable length of time before they came to a clearing with a small log cabin. The scents of mossy earth and wet dog teased her nose, making her suppress a sneeze.

Brian pulled her into a crouched position behind a clump of bushes. "You two stay here while I check out that structure."

Holding on to Scout, she watched as Brian ran in a crouch to the front of the cabin. He moved stealthily, disappearing into the shadows as he worked his way around the structure. She made out the outline of his silhouette as he paused to peer into the windows before he jogged back to her side. "Looks empty. Come on."

She and Scout went with him to the front door. Using his shoulder, he popped the door open, busting the lock.

"This is breaking and entering," she said, hesitating on the threshold of the door.

"We'll pay for damages when this is over. I think these are exigent circumstances."

Not liking the sting of guilt despite knowing the law allowed an officer to make entry to a structure without waiting for permission from the owners to prevent harm to said officer, she walked inside. He shut the door behind her, though it didn't latch because he'd broken the mechanism. She wrinkled her nose at the odor of disuse and mildew. Unable to hold off, she sneezed into the crook of her arm.

Brian's chuckle had her frowning.

"What?" she whispered as she waited for her eyes to adjust to the interior. The windows allowed ambient light to filter through, revealing a small square table with two chairs, two cots and a wood-burning fire stove.

"You sneeze like a kitten."

She crossed the room to the stove. "And you know a lot of kittens that sneeze?"

"One of my stepmothers had cats with babies."

On top of the stove was an oil lamp. Adele searched the shelves lining one wall until she found a box of matches.

"Wait." Brian closed the distance between them and put his hand over hers just as she was about to strike the match. "We shouldn't advertise that we're here."

She set the matches down. "You're right, of course. I just thought some light…"

"I understand." He gave her hand a gentle squeeze before releasing her to search the cabin. "It's okay."

Wrapping her arms around her middle, she tried to contain the chill coursing through her body. "This being on the run is complicated and scary."

TWELVE

"Can't argue with that assessment." Brian pulled out two tubs from beneath a shelf lined with canned goods.

Adele shivered, wishing they were somewhere safe and warm. A tropical vacation where she could stay on dry land and feel the sun on her face. A place where she didn't have to worry about unknown threats and men with guns chasing after her.

"Eureka." He tugged out several pieces of clothing and thrust a pair of pants and a sweatshirt at her. "Change out of your wet clothes. I'll step outside and do the same."

He gathered clothing for himself and went out the door.

On a sigh of resignation, she made short work of changing into the dry, warm, hooded sweatshirt, which was four sizes too big, and sweatpants that she had to roll the top down several times and the bottom hems up. She snuggled into the clothes, grateful to be warm and dry. And safe for the moment.

Scout curled up on the floor and fell asleep.

A few minutes later, Brian knocked softly on the door. Quickly, she tugged the door open. She stifled a giggle. Brian wore a canvas coat, the buttons straining over his broad chest, that rode up on his forearms.

The blue jeans brushed his ankles, clearly the owner of the clothing was much smaller than Brian. He'd taken off his cowboy boots and socks.

"I think we'll start a new fashion trend," he said.

"That's a good look for you."

"This jacket is itchy," he said.

"Maybe there's another sweatshirt," she offered. She rummaged through the tub of clothing, though it was too dark to see colors. Her hands gripped soft, thick material. She held up a shirt, assessing the size. It could work. "A flannel shirt."

She faced Brian as he slipped off the jacket.

Moonlight splashed across his chest, revealing two scars, one on his right pectoral muscle and one on the left side of his abdomen.

Adele swallowed the gasp at the sight of the old injuries. She handed him the flannel shirt.

"Thank you." He turned away, presenting his back and revealing the smooth expanse of skin. But then she noticed his back wasn't smooth at all. He had several rough ridges slicing through the lower half of his skin. He shrugged on the flannel shirt, covering his scars.

Seeing the evidence of his dangerous work filled her with dread and anxiety. "Your scars. Were you shot or knifed?"

He moved to the small table and turned the chair around. Straddling the chair, he folded his arms over the back so the flannel shirt road up, revealing his muscular forearms. "Yes, and yes."

She sat across from him, folding her hands on the dusty surface of the table. "Did you get those wounds protecting a witness?" She held her breath.

"One of them. The others were hunting fugitives."

She didn't want to imagine the situations that had brought the physical damage to his body. "I'm sorry that happened to you."

He shrugged. "Comes with the territory. We all have scars," he said softly. "Even if they aren't visible."

She had her own invisible trauma, and he knew about them now. What hidden injuries did he carry? "You never did answer my question about why you aren't married or at least in a long-term relationship."

For a long moment, he remained silent. "The role models I had of love were not good ones."

"But not every marriage ends in divorce. My parents have been married for nearly forty years."

"They are the exception, not the rule."

"Maybe. But it can happen. And I know there's been hard times for my folks. My mother's illness. My father changed careers several times before landing where he is now. But they always had each other."

"Must be nice to have that example. An example that should tell you that men like Richard Overstreet are few and far between. Not every man will hurt you."

The rapid flutter of her pulse beat in her throat. "You sound like my mother. She's always telling me I need to risk my heart or I will never know what's possible."

"Sage advice."

She reached across the table, putting her hands over his folded ones. He turned his palms up to meet hers. Warmth seeped into her limbs.

"Advice we could both use, no?"

He gave her hands a squeeze. "It's good advice for you." He released her hands and stood. "We should keep moving."

"How far do we have to go?"

"A few miles at least to the road and then we'll follow it back to the house, maybe another three or four miles."

Not sure she could take another step, she asked, "Are we safe here?"

"For now."

She'd take it. "Then can we rest a bit?"

He remained silent for a moment then said, "Yes. Take a cot. I'll stand guard." He picked up his chair and moved to the door, tucking the edge of the high back under the handle. "Won't keep anybody from coming in, but it might slow them down."

She rose and walked to him. Stopping in front of him, their bare feet practically touching. She slipped her arms around his waist and laid her head against his chest. He remained immobile for a moment and then his arms encircled her.

She melted against him. "If I haven't told you lately, I really appreciate all you're doing for me."

"It's my—"

"Job," she finished for him, hating that he kept falling onto those words. She leaned back, looked up into his face. "I know it's your job. But you are also a protector. A guardian and warrior. I've seen the evidence in your actions and in the scars on your body. You don't have to do what you do. But you choose to. And I am grateful." She placed her hand over his heart. "You're a good man."

Shadows covered his face, but she could feel the rapid thump of his heart beneath her palm. His arms tightened, one of his hands sliding up to the back of her neck and tangling in her wet hair. Her breath caught in her chest and held.

He leaned forward, stopping a hair's breadth from kissing her.

Always the gentleman. Her heart thumped. She went on tiptoe, closing the distance between them until their lips met.

He captured her mouth. His lips firm yet gentle. It had been so long since she'd been kissed. He was so strong and sturdy. An anchor in an out-of-control sea. She wanted nothing more than to just stay in this heady sensation, forgetting that the world beyond this little cabin existed.

Finally, he eased away from her and dropped his forehead to meet hers. His breathing was hard and labored. She was glad to know she wasn't the only one affected by the kiss.

"We shouldn't—" he whispered.

Unwilling to let him ruin the moment, she said, "Hush. No regrets."

He lifted his head. The meager light filtering through the dirty windows of the cabin reflected in his eyes. "You're one special woman."

"Thank you." She accepted the compliment, but what she wanted was more. Yet she couldn't ask, wouldn't ask. She disentangled herself from him. "I'll try to get some rest. But you should, too."

"I'll rest when I get you to safety." He stood in front of the window with his back to her.

Wanting nothing more than to step back into the warm comfort of his embrace, she moved to the cot and stretched out on her back. Scout moved from the far side of the cabin to settle down next to the cot. The canvas material was surprisingly comfortable, but knowing Brian and Scout were there, watching over her, gave her peace. She lifted up a quick prayer for safety as she drifted off to sleep.

The moon was high, creating shadows on the ground as Brian stared through the dirty window of the deserted cabin where he and Adele were hiding and searched the inky depths of the forest for a threat.

He could hardly believe that somebody had found his family's lake house and had chased him and Adele away from the safety of the vacation home. It had taken some skill and determination to ferret out the link between Brian and the property belonging to his grandparents. Who were these men? Why were they after the judge?

He'd like to think the fact they'd been able to disable the boat with a well-placed bullet or two was a random fluke but, again, the skills the shooters possessed was high level. Mercenaries for hire?

Discovering that Adele didn't know how to swim had been surprising and concerning. If he'd known, he might not have brought her to a place where it could be necessary for her to be in the water.

He couldn't believe he'd kissed Adele. Or rather, she'd kissed him.

Way to keep things professional.

Adele was such a special woman. Amazing, brave and resilient. His heart thudded in his chest as affection and caring grew. He didn't want these emotions, but he was helpless to ~ his heart from expanding with every moment they spent together. He didn't know what the future could hold for them.

The thought of committing to a relationship filled him with a deep dread, threatening to rob him of his senses. He could not end up like his father and mother. Divorced several times, always thinking the next relationship would be better than the last. He refused to go down that road.

You sound like my mother. She's always telling me I need to risk my heart or I will never know what's possible.

But how could he trust that Adele, or any woman, would ever be fully committed to staying in a relationship? How could he ever take the necessary risk to find out what was possible?

He knew people who had. Gavin Armstrong and his wife, Victoria, had a solid marriage; they had been married for ages. They made it work. Adele's parents made their marriage work. Were they just anomalies? Could he and Adele…

He cut the thought off. Best not to go there. He needed his senses and his judgment to stay sharp. He leaned on the window frame, taking some of the pressure off his back where the scars sometimes ached. Very few people in his life were allowed to see the visible evidence of his job.

Scout rose from his spot beside Adele and stood by the door. He gave a small whine.

Figuring the dog needed to go out, Brian removed the chair from under the door handle. The door swung open slightly.

"Hold," Brian told Scout.

Brian palmed his weapon. If anything happened to Adele's dog, Brian knew she would never forgive him.

After attaching Scout's leash to the dog's collar, Brian toed the door open a little more and waited. When nothing happened, no one attacked or shot at the cabin, he and Scout stepped cautiously outside. Scout let out another little whine. Brian unhooked the leash and Scout took off, disappearing into the bushes.

Standing guard, Brian heard Scout moving through the low underbrush. Then a low growl raised the fine hairs on Brian's nape. Had Scout come across a nighttime critter? Or a more lethal threat?

Pulse jumping, Brian gave a soft whistle, drawing Scout back to the cabin. Halfway to him, the dog stopped and pivoted, his tail standing straight up and ears back. A menacing growl emanated from his throat. Something was out there. Something human?

Brian wasn't going to wait to find out. He gave another short whistle. Scout hesitated then ran to stand beside Brian. Quickly hooking the leash to Scout's collar, Brian hustled them both inside the cabin. He moved to where Adele had curled onto her side on the cot.

Brian put a hand over her mouth and gently shook her. His hand muffled her startled yelp. She blinked up at him.

He whispered, "We have to be on the move, now!"

She nodded. He removed his hand. He didn't relish trucking through the forest on bare feet nor did he want to try to slip his feet into his wet cowboy boots. He went back to the tub full of clothing and found two sets of hiking boots and two pairs of dry socks. After stretching the socks over his feet, he tried both sets of boots, picking one pair that were tight but doable. He thrust the other pair at Adele. "They'll be big. But better than nothing."

While she laced up the boots, Brian rummaged through the cupboards and shelves until he found a box of cereal bars. Unfortunately, there were no bottles of water. He grabbed the box, tucking it under his arm, and gripped the poker. "Let's go."

He went out through the open door first, pausing to let his senses adjust to the night sounds. The absence of noise skated along his flesh like an icy finger. He motioned for Adele, who held Scout's leash, to come out. He used the stars to navigate the correct direction they needed to travel.

Grabbing Adele's hand with his free hand, he led her around to the back of the cabin and into the forest. The boots pinched, and he knew he'd have blisters by the time they reach the lake house. A small price to pay to make sure Adele stayed safe.

Rather than take the dirt road leading to the cabin, they traversed parallel to the road through the thick forest, pushing around underbrush and dodging thick-trunked trees in silence. They each ate a couple of cereal bars for fuel but, without water, the bars only made their thirst more pronounced. Brian kept his senses alert for any out-of-place sound or telltale sign of a threat. The sun rose in the east, casting a barely discernible glow on the horizon to push back the shadows and illuminate the way.

Scout stopped, lifted his nose to the air and turned back the way they had just come.

Heart hammering in his chest, Brian couldn't discern if they were being tracked, but he trusted the dog's keen sense of hearing and smell. Whatever had Scout spooked, be it human or animal, didn't matter. Brian didn't want to find out. They needed to pick up the pace. Adele's energy had waned, her steps slowing. He took Scout's leash from her hand and slipped an arm around her waist.

"Lean on me," he said.

"That's the second time you've told me to lean on you," she said as she allowed him to take some of her weight.

"What can I say, I'm generous that way."

"And I'm grateful. These boots rub."

They continued on as branches scraped at their borrowed clothes. Finally, they came out onto a stretch of highway that would take them back to the lake house. In the distance, headlights roared toward them. Tugging Adele into a crouch, he hid them behind a thick tree trunk and some bushes. He handed Scout's leash back to her. "Stay hidden."

He rose and moved into the road, holding his weapon behind his back with one hand and waving down the approaching vehicle. The bright headlights shone in his eyes, momentarily blinding him as the vehicle screeched to a halt and both the SUV's driver and passenger doors opened. He braced himself.

"Brian!"

Relief flooded his system. Jace and Sera rushed over to him. Brian hugged his friends before he ran back to the brush to get Adele. "Help has arrived."

"I was praying," she said as she stood.

With an arm around her waist, he and Scout escorted her to the road. Sera and Jace hurried them into the SUV.

"Conlan?" Brian asked as soon as they were rolling.

"He's with the boss," Sera told him.

Thankful to know the younger man was safe, Brian leaned against the back seat headrest.

"How did you find us?" Adele asked. She sat next to Brian, Scout's head on her lap while his back paws braced against Brian's thigh.

"Conlan saw the boat stall on the lake," Jace said.

"We all thought maybe you were dead in the boat," Sera said. "We checked and were thankful there was no blood. But bullet holes in the engine. We figured you had to swim to shore.

We've been driving back and forth on as many roads as we could find for the last six hours."

They drove to the lake house, where they gathered their things and changed clothes. Brian hated seeing the destruction from the assault, but he knew it could have been so much worse. Then everyone loaded back into the SUV, and Jace drove them to headquarters.

"There were two of them," Brian told his boss. "Highly trained, with tactical gear and night-vision goggles. The works."

"We saw on the laptop Conlan set up. Their faces were obscured, so we can't ID them. They had gloves on, as well. But you, young lady…" Gavin Armstrong said, pointing to Adele. "You wounded one of them. They tried to wipe up the blood, but we got enough for DNA. The lab will run it against all databases."

"Where do we go from here?" Adele asked.

Gavin turned to his son. "Take them to the ranch."

Jace nodded. "Better give Mom a heads-up."

"Already have. She's expecting the three of you."

Brian stood, facing the two Armstrong men. "Much appreciated."

The Armstrong ranch was under the name of Gavin's wife's family. Though it wouldn't be impossible to trace it to Gavin, it would be much harder because the last names were different, going back several generations.

"When we plugged the leak in this office," Gavin stated, referring to the admin mole planted in the marshal's office by the drug cartel run by Tomas Garcia, "I had every bit of information linking the ranch to me and Jace scrubbed from every database we could find."

"Then what are we are waiting for?" Brian said.

"Head to the roof," Gavin said.

Brian wasn't surprised by the instructions.

Adele slipped her hand into Brian's, causing his heart to swell with emotions that he tamped down. "The ranch?"

"If we're forced to continue to hide, it will be the best place."

Adele's steps faltered as Brian led her to the roof of the US marshals' headquarters building where a helicopter waited on the helipad.

Shielding her face from the wind whipped up by the whirling rotors, she shouted over the rotor noise, "You're joking, right?"

Brian leaned close to say in her ear, "Not at all. This will be the quickest and safest way for us to travel to the ranch."

Her stomach pitched. She'd never been in a helicopter. She'd always imagined her first time would be flying over some beautiful tropical paradise like Kauai or Fiji. Not as a means of escape from unknown assassins. Her blood pounded in her veins. She tightened her hold on Brian's hand. He was her anchor, steadfast and true. And despite her doubts about her own judgment, her feelings for him were growing.

They'd kissed.

It was hard not to relive those moments over and over in her brain. She was amazed she'd even managed any rest after learning of his injuries and feeling so emotionally close to him.

Though they'd escaped the cabin and made it to safety, she hadn't escaped the knowledge she was falling for Brian. Watching him step out onto the road as an unknown car approached had sent her heart into her throat and she'd prayed fervently for his safety. It could've gone so wrong. What if the assassins had been in that car?

But they hadn't been, she had to remind herself. She was safe at Brian's side, and about to climb aboard a helicopter headed to another safe location.

She couldn't help but wonder, though, for how long.

THIRTEEN

Brian helped her into the helicopter's cabin. She settled on the bench seat. He lifted Scout and placed the dog at her feet before climbing in and sitting beside her. He closed and latched the door then handed her a set of headphones. She put them on and adjusted the mic.

"Can you hear me?" he asked into the mic of his headset.

"I can," she said. "Can you hear me?"

"Loud and clear."

As the helicopter rose vertical in the air, she pushed herself against the seatback and hung on to Scout. Once they were clear of the building, the helicopter zoomed forward and, reflexively, she grabbed Brian's hand again.

"Never been in a helicopter?"

Slanting him a wry glance, she said into the headset, "What gave you that idea?"

She heard his chuckle, which eased a little bit

of the tension in her chest. His fingers flexed over hers, giving her comfort and solace.

"Relax. Take in the views."

Her stomach pitched. "Easy for you to say."

She did, however, turn her gaze from the back of the pilot's head to the side window. Despite her nervousness at flying in a small aircraft, she enjoyed the beautiful expanse of the Texas landscape.

The city gave way to rolling hills and flatland dotted with horses and cattle. Her state was beautiful. Seeing it from this vantage point was a new perspective. It seemed, in the past few days, her life had taken on new dimensions. She was grateful, even if the circumstances that had brought her to this point were horrible.

The ride to the ranch lasted no more than twenty minutes and they were setting down in a big pasture filled with scattering horses.

There was a main house painted white with blue shutters. Very inviting. There was also a circle of small cabins surrounding a big fire pit. Several barns lay beyond the cabins. A group of people gathered at the fence line. Brian tugged on her hand, indicating she should follow him out of the helicopter.

Whipping off the headphones, she allowed

him to help her from the flying bird. Scout jumped to the ground easily. Keeping their heads low, they jogged away from the still-rotating rotors. As soon as they were clear, the helicopter lifted off the ground, throwing dust and wind at their backs. The bird took off, flying back the way they'd come until it was just a distant speck in the sky.

They reached the fence line, and Adele was surprised to see ten teenage girls dressed in what Adele would classify as cowboy attire. Boots, jeans, Western-style shirts and cowboy hats in a variety of colors. One of the teens broke away and opened the gate for them to pass through. Scout kept close to Adele.

As Adele smiled at the girl holding the gate, she realized this was not a teenager, but a woman. Petite, with long dark hair and vivid blue eyes. The resemblance to Jace Armstrong was uncanny.

Adele stopped in her tracks. Scout nosed her leg as if to ask what was wrong. Adele thrust out her hand to Gavin Armstrong's wife. "You must be Victoria."

Victoria grasped her hand with a firm handshake. "And you're the judge."

"Adele, please."

Smiling brightly, Victoria gave a nod. "Adele,

it is, then. Welcome to Camp Strong. You'll be safe here."

Adele eyed the teenage girls clustered around her and Brian. Most of them staring at Brian with blatant interest. She didn't blame them. He was a handsome specimen of a man. And dressed in his US marshals' navy windbreaker and a pair of khaki pants, he was even more of a curiosity.

"All right, girls. Back to the barn. Janine," Victoria called out.

One of the older teens stepped forward. She wore jeans, a long-sleeved, plaid shirt and a tan cowboy hat over blond curls. "Yes, ma'am?"

"Teach the girls how to muck the stalls," Victoria instructed.

Janine smiled widely, showing gleaming white teeth. "Yes, ma'am."

There was a collective groan from the other girls. Janine shooed them toward the nearest barn.

"Janine volunteers to help. She lives a couple miles down the road," Victoria explained as she led Adele, Scout and Brian to the main house. "This bunch of teens are foster kids. I've only had them for a few days. But I'll whip them into shape. By the time they leave, they will love horses, get to know Jesus and have a renewed purpose in life."

"So Camp Strong is truly a camp?" Adele said, glancing up at Brian.

"It sure is," Victoria said, pausing on the top step of the porch so that she could look back at Brian and Adele. "Gavin didn't say how long you'll be staying, but I've made up rooms for you. You'll be across the hall from each other. And I've laid out proper attire for you both."

"I hate putting you through all this trouble," Adele said. "Are you okay with Scout being here?"

Victoria held out her hand, urging Adele to take it. Her grip was strong as she gave Adele's hand a pat with her other hand. "You and your dog are most welcome. Our mission at Camp Strong is to help those in need. Gavin has done everything he can to make sure this place is safe." She turned her blue-eyed gaze on Brian. "I understand there was trouble at your lake house."

Brian nodded.

"No one has been able to connect this place to Gavin for nearly thirty years. You don't have to worry."

Brian stepped up onto the porch so that he was even with Victoria. "I should have brought the judge here to begin with."

Adele dropped Victoria's hand and gained the last stair so that she was next to Brian. She nudged him with her shoulder. "You didn't know they would hack the DOJ. This is not your fault." To Victoria, she said, "I want to pull my weight around here. I can help you with the teens or with whatever needs to be done."

"Even mucking out stalls?" Victoria grinned.

"I can," Adele told her in all seriousness. "I spent many summers as a youth at horse camp. I went through a horse crazy phase."

Victoria's grin turned into approval. "Then you will fit right in." Her eyes jumped to Brian. "I hope you still remember the horse lessons I gave you when you were young."

Brian placed a hand over his heart. "You know it."

Victoria opened the front door and walked inside, leaving it open for Adele and Brian to follow.

Adele looked up at Brian. "You came here often when you were young?"

"As I told you, I met Jace when we were kids out at the lake house. I spent several spring breaks here and a few summers, as well."

She would like to see him on a horse, it would complete the whole cowboy image he had going. "I'm really glad you had the Armstrong family in your corner."

"Me, too." The sincere tone in his voice underscored his words.

She stared into his eyes and found herself swaying forward with sharp longing. Attraction flared between them. Would he kiss her?

Deep inside, she acknowledged she wanted him to.

He gave a small shake of his head as he stepped back and gestured for her to precede him inside the house. Tamping down her disappointment, she squared her shoulders as she entered the house, which was as charming inside as outside.

She took in the leather couches, gleaming hardwood floors and bursts of colorful flowers in vases adorning many surfaces.

Victoria led them upstairs and down a hallway. She pointed to one door. "Adele, you're here." Then she pointed to the door across the hall. "Brian, there. The closed door there is the bathroom, which is fully stocked with everything you could need."

Adele opened the door to her room and gave a sigh of pleasure at the clean, crisp lines of blue-and-white bedding. The white walls featured beautifully painted landscapes. On the bed was a stack of clothing and a pink cowboy hat. Suppressing a smile, she turned to Victoria. "You've thought of everything."

"If you're going to be on the ranch, you need a hat. And boots," Victoria replied with a twinkle in her eyes. "I have plenty of sizes for you to try on."

"I don't know what to say or how I'll be able to repay your kindness," Adele said.

"I love to help and I love having guests," Victoria said. "The last person who wore that pink hat was my new daughter-in-law, Abby. Have you met her?"

"No," Adele said. "But I look forward to the day I do."

Victoria patted Adele on the arm. "When you're ready, come on outside. If you're hungry, there are snacks out on the counter for you. Make sure you hydrate. It may be February, but the air is still dry enough to cause havoc with your system."

"Yes, ma'am," Adele and Brian said in unison.

They both laughed. Victoria smiled and walked back downstairs, leaving them alone in the hallway.

"Race to the bathroom?" Adele said. A hot shower sounded marvelous.

Brian opened the door to his room. Over his shoulder, Adele could see the room was appointed in more masculine dark blues and browns. "What kind of gentleman would I be if I deprived you of using the facilities first?"

"You are a gentleman. And I appreciate that. I'll see you downstairs." She grabbed the clothes from the bed and then ducked inside the bathroom, shutting the door.

Leaning back against the hardwood, she smiled. If only they weren't here to hide from assassins and were instead on some kind of cowboy vacation adventure. But they weren't. The danger hunting her was all too real. However, for now, she could at least enjoy being a guest at Camp Strong with Brian at her side.

"Are you limping?" Adele watched as Brian ambled toward her with an awkward gait he hadn't had two days ago when they'd arrived at the ranch.

"I haven't ridden a horse this much since I was a teenager," Brian groused as he joined her in the barn where she was wiping down a beautiful roan named Starburst. They'd just returned from a ten-mile ride with the group of teenage girls staying at Camp Strong. Scout had taken to following Victoria around. The dog's affections were fickle.

"You know stretching would take care of that."

He snorted. "I exercise. Lift weights. Run."

"But do you stretch before and after? I do a set routine in the morning and a short routine at night before I go to bed. Keeps me limber."

Brian seemed to choke on his own spit. He spun on his heels and headed for a stall. "I'm going to muck out this stall. Over here."

Adele watched him pick up a shovel, a bucket, and disappear inside an empty stall. Patting Starburst, she said, "I wonder what has him all upset?"

He was going to be even more anxious when she reminded him about tomorrow. She walked the short distance to where Brian was cleaning the stall. The sound of the metal shovel scraping across the concrete pad beneath the straw and debris left by the horse grated on her nerves.

She leaned against the stall opening. Watching the way his muscles beneath his shirt bunched and moved with his effort was enthralling. The man was strong and handsome. A good man with a big heart. "Is there something troubling you?"

He paused, resting his hands on the top of the shovel. "As a matter of fact... Somebody's trying to kill you. We're stuck here on a ranch with a bunch of teenage girls who giggle way too much. This isn't a vacation. And—" He turned away from her and began shoveling again.

"And what?"

Pausing again, but not turning to look at her, he said, "Look. This isn't some reality break from our lives. We need to keep things professional. And it's really difficult when we're so cooped up."

She stared at his broad back. The blue chambray shirt hid the scars she knew marked his skin. "We were out in the open for the last few hours. How can you say we've been cooped up?"

He pivoted to face her. "Look. I like you. Way more than I should. We kissed. That can't happen again."

A flush of excitement and confusion filled her veins. Was he saying he wanted to kiss her again? "Why not?" She pushed away from the stall door and walked toward him. "I like you, too. That's not a crime. We're both adults. It's okay to like each other."

He set the shovel against the wall and stepped past her to walk down the center aisle of the horse barn, the heels of his worn cowboy boots echoing on the concrete.

Stunned that he'd just walk away had her blood boiling. Grabbing onto the pink cowboy hat on her head, she hurried to catch up to him. "Brian, I don't understand. What's gotten into you?"

"You." He made a gesture with his hand encompassing the whole camp. "This place."

Still not grasping his strange behavior, she said slowly, "Okay, I get it. You're a man of action. This waiting is really hard for you. But you don't need to be rude and snap my head off about it."

Brian halted and scrubbed a hand over his face. "I'm sorry. I just need some space."

"Fine. Space you can have." Not understanding him at all but extremely irritated by his insufferable vagueness, Adele went into the barn. But she paused. What was she doing? Letting his disgruntled mood chase her back inside?

She whirled around, finding Brian still standing there, staring after her. She marched up to him and got right in his face. "Tomorrow is Richard Overstreet's parole hearing. I'm going. Make it happen."

Once again, she marched away from him and into the barn, but this time it was on her terms.

She heard him call out, "As you wish."

She fisted her hands and ducked into the nearest stall. She kicked at the clean piles of wood shavings covering the floor. She didn't understand him, would never understand him. Men! He was not her problem. She needed to get through tomorrow. Why hadn't the marshals, the FBI, the ATF and the rest of the alphabet soup agencies found out who wanted her dead?

This wasn't fair.

Someone was trying to kill her. Brian was acting so weird. She was falling for the man. Her breath hitched. Was she really?

Yes.

So not fair.

A small voice inside her head whispered, *God never promised life would be fair. Only that He would be with you.*

She took a few calming breaths, hanging on to that sentiment as she returned to grooming Starburst. "At least you want my company."

Maybe she needed to stick with animals rather than men. So much less complicated.

Brian paced on the back porch of the ranch house. He'd changed for dinner into clean jeans, clean boots and a Western-style plaid shirt. A fresh Stetson sat on his head. He paused every once in a while to look out at the camp scene where the teenage girls scurried back and forth from their cabins to the facilities. He watched them morph from grubby horsewomen into cleaned-up young ladies who looked more like they were ready to go out on the town than to have dinner in the main house with the family.

Coming here had been a mistake. It had been a mistake for his boss to assign him to protect Adele. It had been a mistake taking her to the lake house. It was all one big giant mistake. He should've let Sera take over when she'd offered.

But deep inside, Brian acknowledged letting anyone else take over hadn't been an option. Not because he didn't trust his friends and colleagues. He did, implicitly.

No, the reason he'd agreed to the assignment, the reason he hadn't let Sera take over, was that he was falling for Adele and he was helpless to stop it.

He didn't want these feelings crowding his chest. He didn't want the glimmer of hope for a future where they could be together.

She thought her judgment was faulty when it came to men. What about his judgment? Would he end up like his parents, married and divorced so many times he'd lose count?

He wasn't going down that road. The best way not to, was to never start.

It ate at him that they hadn't been able to discover who wanted Adele dead. They had gone through her files and given a long list of names to the FBI, ATF, DEA and their own tech expert. No suspect jumped out as the culprit. Many of the names on the list either alibied out, had already passed from this world or were just too far away to be the one wreaking havoc on Adele's life.

That didn't mean it couldn't still be Garcia. Or someone in the cartel hoping to stop the proceedings. Sera had said she had several leads on finding Maria Montoya but, so far, nothing had panned out. The daughter of Tomas Garcia was exceptionally good at evading law enforcement. Brian's gut clenched. Did she have someone in the San Antonio PD or FBI, ATF, DEA—or the marshals service who was feeding her intel?

What about Overstreet's brother? A military man who would definitely have the know-how to build a bomb. But, according to Gavin, Trevor Overstreet had been on base when the courthouse blew up and when the explosive device had been planted beneath their SUV.

And then there was Ortega. What was up

with the senator? He had been hounding the US marshals since the moment they'd taken Adele away from her home, wanting to know where she was and if she was safe. According to Gavin, John Ortega was becoming more and more insistent that he know where she was. Because he really had feelings for her?

Gavin and Jace had interviewed everyone in Ortega's office, and no one knew anything about giving a courier an envelope full of anthrax. That didn't mean one of them couldn't be lying. They just had no proof. But why would Ortega want to hurt Adele? It didn't make sense. What did make sense was that Ortega was controlling and he wanted Adele for himself. Brian was not going let that happen.

Yeah, right, like Brian had any control over what happened to Adele once this assignment was over.

But Brian did want control. Well, not control necessarily; but he wanted to be a part of her life, which was not going to happen.

"You are going to wear a hole in my deck," Victoria said as she came out the back door.

Brian halted abruptly. "Sorry, ma'am."

"What's eating at you?" Victoria cocked her head and pinned him with her gaze. "I'm a good listener. And I'm told I give good advice."

Brian had no doubt that Victoria, who had a degree in psychology and at one time had been a family counselor, would be able to give him good advice. He just wasn't ready to share all the fuzzy emotions clouding his thoughts.

Victoria gave him a little smile and stepped to the railing so that he had a side view of her. She was a beautiful woman. Petite with dark hair held in a braid down her back. Jace got a lot of his good looks from his mother.

"I think I can guess what's going on with you." Victoria turned to face him.

Brian wanted to squirm under that intense stare. Even if Victoria barely reached his shoulder, she was an intimidating woman when she wanted to be. He waited, silently wary of what she might say.

"You care for the judge. But you're letting what your parents modeled for you be the litmus test of how relationships work. They were broken people. Though, to be fair, we all are broken in some ways, but you aren't like your parents."

"Thanks." He wasn't sure what to make of her statement. There were times when he felt broken beyond repair.

"Trust yourself. Trust the judge. Personally, I trust both of you." She walked to the door and opened it, but paused to say, "Please, go tell the teens dinner is about to be served."

Brian groaned. "Do I have to?"

"What are you, twelve?" Victoria grinned. "You're not afraid of some teenage girls, are you? No wonder you're afraid of the judge."

"I'm not afraid of the judge." Far from it. The teenagers, however, had him shaking in his boots. The gaggle of girls was like a group of gnats flying around, giggling and whispering. It was unnerving.

Victoria shook her head and stepped inside. Brian hesitated on the first stair leading down toward the teenager camp. The door behind him opened again. He swiveled to find Adele. His breath caught. She wore a long-sleeved frilly dress that hung to the tops of her borrowed cowboy boots. A belt at her waist accentuated her curves. Her auburn hair was loose about her shoulders and the slight sheen on her lips drew his gaze.

"I hear you need some help?"

His chest expanded and he held out his hand. "That, I do."

FOURTEEN

After a rowdy and giggly dinner, Brian's ears would never be the same. The only male in the room, he had quietly listened to all the girls chatter. He escaped as soon as he could to the front porch, far from the hubbub, and relished the quiet of the Texas night. The February air was cool but not biting. He sat on the porch swing and gripped the chain in his hand.

The door opened and Adele stepped out. "May I join you?"

His heart leapt into his throat. Unable to form words, he patted the seat next to him.

"Don't mind if I do." Adele gingerly sat on the swing. She tried to make it rock but his planted feet prevented the swing from doing its job.

"Do you mind?" She nudged his feet with her own. He lifted his boots off the floor enough to allow the swing to rock gently forward and back. The rhythm was both soothing and distressing. For a flash of a moment, he could see them as an old married couple, sitting on the porch just like this, watching the night sky.

"I hate to bring this up," she said. "What's the plan for tomorrow?"

Whatever peace he'd felt dissipated. "I talked at length with Gavin and Jace and Sera. We have a plan. We will leave the ranch the way we came in. By helicopter. We'll go to headquarters."

"Good to know. This time I'll take some antinausea medicine."

He reached for her hand and gave it a squeeze. "You'll be fine. You did well on the way here."

She turned her hand so that their palms matched and her fingers wrapped through his. His heart tugged with tenderness and his conscience whispered he should let go, but he couldn't bring himself to break the contact. He liked holding her hand. He liked the way they fit together. He liked her. More than liked.

You care about the good judge. Victoria's voice rang through his head.

Yes, he did.

"So how do we go from the headquarters office to where the hearing is being held?"

"Sera's going to dress up like you and go out the front door, get into an official caravan, and they will drive her away, while you and I will put on disguises and go out the back door."

"That sounds like a very good plan."

"You can thank Sera," he said. "My idea was to pressure the justice system to move the parole hearing. But the parole board wouldn't bend."

"Well, they do have protocols. But I am surprised they wouldn't postpone. Truth be told, I'm more surprised there's even a hearing. Richard must have a good lawyer."

"You could not go," Brian said.

"Avoiding the situation won't make it go away."

His respect for her grew. She was an amazing person. He stood and pulled her to her feet. "We should probably get some rest."

She wrapped her arms around his waist and laid her head against his chest. Brian didn't even try to fight the longing to wrap her in his embrace.

After a moment, she stepped back. "I know you want to keep things professional, unemotional, between us. But right now, you're my anchor. Can you continue to be that?"

"I can be that." And so much more. His heart squeezed tight.

"Good. Tomorrow is going to be very hard for me. I need to know I can count on you."

"Whatever you need."

Seeming satisfied with his answer, she disappeared inside the house, leaving him wondering if she asked for his heart, would he be able to resist?

The next day, after the helicopter had transported Adele and Brian from the ranch to the marshals' headquarters in San Antonio, Adele was fitted with a flak vest and a US marshals' windbreaker. She was dressed as the other marshals were. A baseball cap with the marshals' logo hid most of her hair. She didn't usually wear hats, the sensation was unfamiliar and uncomfortable. She'd used bobby pins Sera had given her to keep the shorter strands of hair tucked beneath the brim of the ball cap. Dark sunglasses covered her eyes, and the khaki pants were a bit too big, but a belt held them up.

Sera was the only one not wearing the standard-issue attire. Posing as Adele, Sera wore a wig with long red hair to hide her face, and a judge's robe to hide the flak vest and tactical gear beneath.

Stomach churning with worry, Adele struggled to believe this was going to work. Sera was taller than she was. Not to mention her skin tone was much more sun-kissed. Sera slipped on a pair of big sunglasses, which did a good job of hiding her dark eyes and most of her cheeks.

The plan was simple enough and, if all went well, would work. Or so Brian assured Adele. Sera and the convoy were going to the make-shift courthouse after an announcement went out this morning via the media that Judge Weston would be taking the bench.

Once Sera and the convoy left, Brian and Adele would slip out the back, walk across the street and down to the federal building a block away from the burned courthouse. There the parole hearing would be held.

Brian had already confirmed that Richard Overstreet had been transported to the jail in the basement of the federal building.

Adele hadn't been joking when she'd told Brian this would be hard for her. Facing Richard again after all these years and reliving those moments was not something she wanted to do. But she was certain the threats on her own life had nothing to do with Richard. Why wouldn't somebody have ambushed the transport and tried to orchestrate an escape for Richard? That would have been easier than trying to kill a district court judge.

"All right, people." Gavin Armstrong addressed the twenty or so US marshals assembled in the room. "Look lively. Make a big show of getting the judge to the SUV. I want lights and sirens. I want all eyes on the convoy while Brian and Adele go out the back."

There was a murmur of agreement as everybody filed out of the armory, escorting Sera, to the convoy, leaving Brian and Adele and Gavin and one other man behind.

"This is Lucas Cavendish." Gavin introduced the man who was dressed in casual clothing. His square jaw was covered in trimmed long stubble, his hair hung longer than what one would expect a US marshal to have. "Lucas agreed to come aboard and help us today. He just transferred in from Florida."

Brian shook the man's hand. "Glad to have you on our team."

Lucas gave Brian a chin nod. "I'll have your back." To Adele, the man turned his deep gray eyes on her and gave her a very deferential nod. "Your Honor."

"Thank you, Deputy Cavendish."

"You can call me Caveman," Lucas said. "My military call name. Still getting used to the whole 'deputy marshal' title." He slanted a glance at Gavin.

"Lucas has only been on the job for six months. He's a marine gunnery sergeant"

"Florida didn't work out?" Brian asked with a wary note in his voice.

Adele's own anxiety ratcheted up with the question. She held her breath as she waited for the answer.

"Something like that."

Apparently, Lucas wasn't big on talking. Adele wanted to know the man's story. If he was going to help protect her, she at least deserved to know why he wasn't still on his original post. "Can you elaborate?"

Lucas and Gavin exchanged a glance. Gavin gave a nod.

"I was part of a joint task force with ATF. We brought down an arms dealer in Miami. My cover was blown. I needed to get out of there fast. All the players think I'm dead."

Somewhat mollified, Adele nodded. "Thank you for letting us know."

Gavin looked at his watch. "Get a move on. You two walk over. Lucas will follow."

"Why not drive?" Adele asked.

"Access to the federal building is limited due to construction," Gavin said. "It would draw more attention if we allowed just your vehicle through, thus defeating the purpose of the decoy."

Her nerves jangled and her courage at facing Richard faltered. Could she do it?

Putting a hand to Adele's lower back, Brian urged her forward.

Her feet felt cemented to the floor. It took all her inner strength to walk with Brian.

Adele was thankful for the sunglasses as they stepped outside the US marshals' building. The February sun was low in the sky. A few drops of rain pinged off the weatherized jacket she wore. She was thankful for its warmth as the wind blew, sneaking beneath the collar.

They went to the corner and waited for the light. Adele could feel the tension coming off Brian. And Lucas, for that matter. The man casually followed, seeming to be minding his own business, but Adele could sense his alert gaze searching the buildings' rooflines. She shuddered. Did he expect a sniper?

The light turned and they crossed the street, starting down the walkway past a building under construction. A strange noise rent the air and bits of concrete exploded near her feet, biting into her shins.

Someone was shooting at them.

"Shooter. Southwest corner of the Dunlap building." Lucas Cavendish, aka Caveman, yelled to Brian as he raced across the street to the building entrance.

Heart pumping with adrenaline, Brian

grabbed Adele, positioning her in front of him as he hustled her toward the boarded-up entrance of the building under construction to their right. At the doorway, he lifted his foot and kicked the thin planks of board inward, splintering wood and creating an opening. Bullets imbedded into the doorframe next to his head.

Ducking, he propelled Adele inside. More gunfire hit the structure, barely missing them and creating holes in the concrete floor. Brian swerved to the left, taking Adele with him and then steering her to the right as more shots penetrated the walls of the building, landing too close for comfort. There was no time for him to return fire. Brian secured Adele behind a steel beam. She flattened her back against the wide metal holding up the ceiling and wrapped her arms around his waist as he stood in front of her, his chest heaving.

"We can't stay here," he managed to say past the constriction tightening his lungs. "We need to move."

"Why?" she asked. "Caveman and the other marshals will get the shooter. We just have to hold out and stay behind this beam."

What she said sounded logical. But alarm bells rang in his head. How had the shooter known they would be using the back exit? Why hadn't the shooter gone after the decoy? Was there another mole in the US Marshals Service?

The sound of metal against concrete came from behind him, sending a jolt of fear down his spine. He spun. Long sheets of plastic hung from the ceiling where walls once stood. He could make out the outline of commercial electrical equipment. A shadow moved. Someone was back there.

Brian grabbed his cell phone and hit the speed dial number for his boss. He held the phone to his ear and said in a hushed voice, "Active shooter. Building under construction."

"Roger."

Brian hung up. To the right was a set of stairs going to the second floor.

Until help arrived and he knew what was going on, he needed to secure the judge. Protecting her was paramount. Not only because of the job but because he loved her. The realization smacked him in the solar plexus. But he couldn't deal with his revelation. He tucked it far away from his mind so he could concentrate on protecting Adele.

He slid his hands down Adele's arms and grasped her hands. Capturing her gaze, he said, "See that staircase? When I say run, I want you to move as fast as you can. Don't look back. I'll be right behind you."

Her eyes widened, but she nodded.

Satisfied she would do as he asked, he said, "On three."

She squeezed his hand, letting him know she understood.

"One…two…three… Run!"

They ran for the stairs.

Bullets tore through the hanging plastic sheets and disintegrating drywall in explosions of white dust. The pinging of bullets chased them up the stairs. He braced himself, figuring it would be only a matter of time before he took a bullet. Better him than Adele.

He let go of Adele's hand to enable her to move quicker. "Go."

The sound of running feet pounded in his skull. Brian followed Adele up the stairs, taking the stairs two at a time. He put his hand at the small of Adele's back, urging her to move faster. They reached the second-floor landing and a long hallway where many of the rooms were just skeletal beams.

He grabbed Adele's hand. "Come on."

They ran down the hall, searching for somewhere to hide. He didn't want to get boxed into a closed space. But they needed shelter. Somewhere he could take a stand. The heavy foot-falls of somebody coming up the stairs echoed through the under-construction building. In the distance, sirens wailed. Hope bloomed that his fellow officers would arrive soon.

A singsong voice rang out, "I know you're in here. You can't get away. You *won't* get away."

Adele gasped, her breath coming fast. Her hand shook within his grasp. He pulled her behind a partition and gripped her by the shoulders. "Stay strong. Don't give in to the panic. Not yet."

She nodded, her whole-body quaking with the effort to control her anxiety. He reached into his ankle holster and produced a .32-caliber handgun, thrusting the small piece into her hands.

She recoiled, but he wrapped his hands around hers, keeping the muzzle down.

"Keep your finger off the trigger unless you're going to fire," he told her in a hushed tone. "But I want you to be equipped to defend yourself if I'm not able to."

Horror shone bright in her wide eyes. "Don't say that. Don't you dare—"

Her concern for him wrapped around his heart. He dipped his head for a quick, deep kiss. He didn't have time to relish the sensations or to acknowledge that she kissed him back. They had to keep moving, staying stationary could get them killed. He didn't want to die. And he wouldn't let her die. He sent a prayer heavenward for safety.

There was another staircase directly opposite them. But if they ran across the hall, their pursuer could pick them off. A concrete saw caught his attention.

He leaned in close to Adele and whispered in her ear, "When I say run, you go up the staircase."

"What are you going to do?" she whispered back.

"Create a diversion." He turned her to face the staircase. "Remember. When I say *run*. Don't hesitate. I'll be right behind you."

He moved away from her, grabbed the concrete saw and stretched it out as far as the extension cord would go. He moved past the point where Adele stood hidden by a partition. They locked eyes. He gave a nod. Her trusting wide-eyed stare had his heart rate doubling.

He flipped on the power switch and the high-pitched whine of the saw filled the cavernous building. He couldn't hear the gunman now. Holding the saw at arm's length, his muscles bunched at the vibration of the blade rattling up his arm. On a breath, he set the saw on the ground and stepped back as the tool ate away at the concrete with a horrific grating noise that jarred through him and set his teeth on edge.

Bullets whizzed by his head. He dove to the side, rolled and shouted, "Run!"

He prayed Adele heard him over the sound of the concrete saw cutting away at the floor, spitting bits of debris and dust into the air. Brian drew his Glock and rolled to land behind a beam. He brought his gun up at the ready. On a breath, he peered around the metal beam. He could see the gunman. Dark tactical gear covered his body. A face mask and military combat helmet covered his head. Definitely military or mercenary. Like the men who'd assaulted the lake house. Hired guns. But who was the one behind the attacks?

The gunman raised his automatic rifle and sprayed bullets at Brian. Ducking back behind the beam, Brian flattened himself on the ground and returned fire, shooting the gunman in the shin. The man went down, bullets spraying the ceiling as he fell. Brian hopped to all fours. He didn't debate whether he should subdue the gunman or go after Adele. Her safety was his priority.

Brian jumped to his feet and checked the partition. He was glad to see she had heard him. He ran for the stairs as more bullets whizzed past him. He glanced over his shoulder. For a moment, he thought maybe he had double vision. He saw double. Two gunmen. One helping the other to his feet. He'd made the right call in not subduing the gunman because his cohort would have caught Brian by surprise and finished him off.

Brian took the stairs two at a time while using his cell phone. "Two gunmen. One suspect wounded but not disabled. Asset on third floor."

Static echoed in his ear then his boss's voice came on the line. "On the way. ETA two min."

On the third-floor landing, Brian skidded to a halt. The remodeling hadn't reached this area. Closed doors lined both sides of the hallway. Brian pushed open the first door. The office space was empty. He moved to the next one. Also empty. He hurriedly moved down the hall, checking each room. The fifth door opened to a dark room filled with office furniture.

"Adele?" he whispered.

"Brian?" Her voice came from behind a large credenza.

Brian entered and quietly shut the door. He hurried across the room and peered around the side of the credenza. Adele was squatted, the .32 in her hands.

"Muzzle down," he told her.

She angled the barrel at the floor. "Is it safe?"

"No." He held out his hand. "We need to get out of here. We'll be sitting ducks if we stay."

The sound of doors being opened alerted Brian that it was too late. If they left the room now, it would be too easy for the gunmen to take them out. They needed to make a stand until backup arrived.

"Back to the credenza," he told Adele.

She shuffled backward, making herself small behind the credenza. He went around to the other side and lifted the credenza up, swinging it out to accommodate his bulk. He set the piece of furniture gently down and hunkered behind it, too.

Into his phone he said, "Trapped on third floor. Fifth room from stairs." He turned the phone off. He could only pray with all his might that his fellow US marshals would arrive before it was too late.

Cold shivers of fear ravaged Adele's body. How had the sniper escaped from Deputy Cavendish? Was the deputy in on it?

She was glad she had left Scout with the

receptionist at the US Marshals Service. If something happened to him… If something happened to Brian…

She took a shuddering breath, doing all she could to keep the anxiety from overwhelming her. Nausea roiled in her gut. The ambient light sneaking around the boarded-up windows seemed to fade to a pinpoint with fuzzy edges. She was going to faint. She tucked her head between her knees and took deep breaths. Brian's hand settled on her back, soothing up and down.

In her ear he whispered, "Breathe. When they come through that door, just stay down. If one of them approaches from your side, shoot. It doesn't matter where you aim. Just shoot, until there are no more bullets."

If he was trying to calm her down, his words were doing the exact opposite. She'd never fired a gun before. She'd never been in a situation like this before, either.

Inhaling, she rallied a prayer, asking God to protect them. To get them out of this predicament.

FIFTEEN

The door to the room burst open, slamming back against the wall. Adele jumped and stifled a yelp.

"Come out, come out, wherever you are," a deep masculine voice coaxed.

"Stop playing," the other gunman admonished his partner. "We need to get in and get out."

"Come on, it's more fun this way," the first man said. "I like to see them sweat."

"You're sick, bro."

"No more than you."

The men's voices sounded like they were closing in. Adele raised her gun, holding it in front of her. But would the men come around the side? Or would they come from above. She pressed herself against the wall, steadying her hands.

Deep within the building, the sounds of agents arriving was a welcomed echo bouncing off the walls. There were shouted orders. The thunder of pounding feet coming up the stairs.

"Bro, we got to go."

"We finish this," the man with the deep voice said in a harsh tone.

Adele held her breath.

"Are you crazy? I'm out of here."

In the next instant, Brian jumped up, squeezing the trigger on his weapon, the deafening sound reverberating off the walls and jolting through Adele. She cringed, trying to get away from the noise of violence. She heard thuds.

Then she heard voices.

"Halt! Drop your weapons!" Marshal Gavin Armstrong's voice rang out.

"Securing suspect number one." Jace's voice reached Adele and she sagged in relief.

"Suspect number two secure." Sera's voice held a hard edge.

Brian placed his hand on her shoulder. "It's safe now."

He reached around her and took his gun back. She was thankful to be done holding the weapon.

He moved to help her to her feet. She swayed and he snaked an arm around her waist, providing her an anchor. Her vision swam. She watched the US marshals drag the two gunmen to their feet.

"You okay?" Gavin asked.

"We're good, boss," Brian told him.

"Sorry for the delay," Gavin said. "The sniper had the building rigged with explosives. It was a tense scene and delayed our response time."

"I understand." The welfare of innocents had to be considered.

Jace ripped the helmet off the gunman and exposed his face.

Adele stared at the man. "Brian, he looks like an older version of Richard's brother. The ones from the picture in the Overstreet house."

Sera removed the face covering from the second shooter.

Astonishment cascaded through Adele. Twins. Did Irene Overstreet know her son wasn't dead? Was she aware of what they were doing, trying to kill Adele to keep her from testifying at Richard's parole hearing?

"Apparently, Irene Overstreet was wrong. Her son wasn't dead, after all," Brian murmured. "Let's get out of here."

Brian held on to Adele, giving her support as they made their way to street level. She blinked her eyes at the bright sunlight. She looked across the parking lot to where Lucas had another man in tactical gear handcuffed.

Obviously, the Overstreet brothers had hired another shooter.

Adele was glad to know her earlier fear that "Caveman" Cavendish might be one of the gunmen was unfounded. She let out a relieved breath.

Brian cupped her elbow and started across the street, back toward the US marshals' building.

"No," she said, breaking away from him. "I need to get to the federal building. These men tried to stop me from testifying. I'm not going to let them succeed."

Brian paused. "You're sure you're up for going in front of the parole board?"

"I am," she said. It was time to face her past and put it behind her. She'd learned long ago that avoiding painful situations only led to more pain.

"Okay. You're the boss," Brian said with a grin.

She smiled, thinking not too long ago he'd said she wasn't the boss of him. So much had happened since that day.

He pulled out his phone. "I'll let Gavin know." He dialed and then spoke into the phone. "I need to get the judge over to the federal building." He listened then said, "Much obliged." He hung up. "Gavin and Jace will head over after they process the Overstreet brothers and their pal."

Gratitude filled Adele. She smiled up at Brian. "Thank you."

"Of course." Putting his hand on the small of her back, he guided her along the sidewalk, and they hurried to the entrance of the federal building.

At the metal detectors, Brian showed his badge and was let through. Since she didn't have a badge, she had to remove the belt from her waist, the bobby pins from her hair and the US marshals' ball cap she'd been given. Once she was cleared, she tucked the bobby pins into the pocket of the pants, deciding it didn't matter if she had strands of hair escaping the cap, which she put back on her head because her hair was undoubtedly a mess. They took the stairs to the hearing room on the second floor.

Adele's steps slowed as Senator John Ortega came into view, along with his security detail comprised of three men in black suits.

She locked stares with John.

His brown eyes grew wide and he hurried toward them. He was impeccably dressed, as always, in a charcoal pinstripe suit, white dress shirt and red power tie. "Adele, what are you doing here?" His gaze bounced to Brian. "Deputy, explain yourself."

Beside her, Brian stiffened. "The judge is testifying in a parole hearing."

Something flashed deep in John's eyes, but he quickly banked what Adele could only describe as anger mixed with confusion. "I don't understand. What case could you be testifying to today?"

"Richard Overstreet's parole hearing," she told him.

John's expression went blank. "I didn't know you were involved in this case."

"Really?" All he'd had to do was to read the case file to know that she was Overstreet's victim. A flutter of anxiety started low in her belly. "What are you doing here?"

John looked at Brian and then back to Adele with a frown. "I am here on behalf of a friend."

"What friend?" Brian asked, his voice hard.

The senator's gaze narrowed. "That is my business."

Brian's phone rang. He checked the caller ID. "It's Sera." He turned to Adele. "Stay put." He took a couple of steps away to talk to his colleague.

John turned to Adele. "Are you all right? You've a smudge on your face. And why are you wearing a US Marshals' windbreaker and hat?"

Suddenly self-conscious, she touched the brim of the cap. She'd forgotten she wore the thing.

"There's a restroom there," John said, pointing to the women's room. "Why don't you freshen up?"

Adele's gaze shot to Brian. She gestured toward the bathroom. He nodded.

She turned on her heels and went into the restroom. Taking the cap off, she shook out her hair and finger-combed it into some semblance of order. She splashed water on her face and used a paper towel to remove the smudges from her face. What she wouldn't give for a shower and a massage. When this ordeal was over, she promised herself some pampering.

"You can do this," she told herself in the mirror. "Stay strong."

The door to the restroom opened and one of the men in John's security detail walked in.

She frowned at him through the mirror. "You're in the wrong room."

Then she noticed the gun with the silencer in his hand.

Her heart rate jackknifed in her chest.

"Scream," he said, "and I drop you where you stand."

* * *

"Be careful, friend," Brian said into the phone. He was glad to hear Sera had a lead on Maria Montoya, the woman they believed had taken over Tomas Garcia's cartel. Sera was leaving town to join a joint task force with DEA and ATF.

He hung up and headed for the woman's restroom where Adele had disappeared to. Why was she taking so long? Was she having second thoughts about testifying?

"Deputy," Senator Ortega called to him.

Brian stopped to face the other man, noting his security detail, which had fanned out earlier, had moved closer. And one of the guards was missing. "Senator."

"I have friends in the service who've kept me apprised of the good work you've been doing to keep Adele safe," Ortega said in a mild tone.

Yet Brian had the feeling Ortega wasn't at all happy. There was something going on here. Why was the senator at the federal building, in front of the room being used for Overstreet's parole hearing? Why weren't there more people around? Why was there no media? It had seemed to Brian that Ortega used every opportunity he could to plant himself in front of a camera.

Then the first part of Ortega's sentence slammed into Brian's mind like a sledgehammer. Someone within the marshals service had been talking to the senator. A rush of anger had Brian narrowing his gaze on Ortega. "What aren't you telling us?"

Something dark slithered through Ortega's gaze and he gave a smile that was all politician-smooth. "What makes you think I'm hiding something?"

Hmm. Was the senator feeling guilty? Doubtful. The man oozed confidence. "A gut feeling."

"That's too bad." He gave a slight nod to his security detail.

Brian's internal threat meter pinged on high. He put his hand on his weapon as the two bodyguards moved in, flanking Brian.

"Don't do that," Ortega said, gesturing to Brian's sidearm, which was already halfway out of the holster. "We don't want to get messy in here."

Reluctantly, Brian lifted his hand off his weapon. One of the senator's men relieved Brian of his Glock, then quickly searched him. He found the .32 strapped to his ankle. Brian held his breath, praying the guy didn't check the inside of his boot where he kept a small knife hidden.

When the man straightened, tucking both of Brian's weapons in the waistband of his trousers, Brian asked Ortega, "What's going on?" His gaze bounced to the closed door of the restroom. Was Adele okay?

"These two gentlemen are going to escort you and the good judge somewhere safe."

As if on cue, the door to the restroom opened. Adele stepped out, her eyes wide, the expression on her face a mix of shock and horror. Behind her, the missing member of the three-man security detail stepped out, holding a gun to the back of her head.

Brian's gaze sought the buildings cameras, hoping that all of this was being recorded. He spied one in the corner to his left.

With his breath lodged in his chest, Brian's eyes snapped to the senator. "You're behind the threats against the judge?"

A slight sneer curled Ortega's lip. "I am."

His glance strayed to the camera then returned to Ortega. "You won't get away with this."

Ortega laughed. "Do you think I'm stupid enough to do something that would be caught on camera and incriminate me?" He gestured to the camera in the corner. "All video surveillance in the building and on the block were disabled before I arrived. No one other than the parole hearing board will know I was here. I've taken measures to ensure I'm safe from public scrutiny." His gaze moved to Adele as she halted beside Brian. "If you had stayed away like planned, you'd be safe, too."

"John, I don't understand. You're a senator. You're bound by law, and the oaths you took, to protect the state and its citizens. Why are you doing this?" Adele asked. The shock and fear in her voice rang clear.

Brian wished he could wrap his arms around her and tell her it would be okay. But, deep inside, he didn't think that Ortega was going to let them live. Where was his boss and Jace? They should be here any moment. He just needed to buy time.

"The judge deserves to know what's going on," Brian stated, hoping to keep the man talking. He liked to preen, so let him preen.

Ortega shrugged. "I guess it won't matter. Soon, this will be done and the whole situation will be taken care of."

Meaning the elimination of him and Adele. Brian could only imagine how hard it was for Adele to hold on to the anxiety that had to be swamping her when a flood of angst was filling his veins.

"Richard Overstreet is my son. His mother,

Irene, and I had an affair when I was still just an up-and-coming lawyer. She told me she'd lost the child." His tone held a note of sadness.

Brian knew the man hadn't had any children with his ex-wife.

Ortega's expression hardened. "I didn't know about Richard until six months ago when Irene came to see me. She's ill, as you know, and she wanted her son out of prison before she died. She has proof he's my son. She'd somehow obtained DNA samples and compared them." His lips twisted with distaste. "Things would be so much different if she'd told me the truth when she had my son."

"You're here to plead on Richard's behalf?" Adele asked. "Do you know what he did?"

Ortega slanted her a harsh glance. "If I'd had a chance to raise him, he wouldn't have done those horrible things. But she chose to keep him from me."

"You don't know if that's true," Adele countered.

Brian was proud of her for pushing back.

"Maybe, maybe not. But he's done enough time," Ortega said.

"So your plan was to do away with Adele." The puzzle pieces fit together, even if they were warped.

"Not my plan. Irene's other boys." Ortega shook his head. His gaze implored Adele to understand. "I just wanted you to stay far from the hearing until it was over."

Disgust crossed Adele's face. "But you went along with their plot to kill me."

"I didn't like it. I still don't," Ortega said. "I thought if I could just keep you from testifying, I could go in and talk on behalf of Richard. I could get him released for Irene. I could save my career." He gave Brian a sullen look. "But you had to interfere."

"Not sorry to have thwarted your plans," Brian said. "Now what are you going to do?"

"I'm going into that hearing to plead on behalf of Richard. He's been an exemplary inmate these past fifteen years."

"You pushed for him to have the hearing," Adele said. "His minimum sentencing isn't even up."

"Yes, I advocated for the hearing. But he did the hard work of turning his life around while inside." His eyes glittered with malice. "I will not let you ruin me."

"Why not go to the governor and ask for a pardon?" Brian asked. His gaze went to the door, hoping to see Gavin and Jace. Where were they?

Ortega gave a dry chuckle. "Sorry, Deputy, no one is coming to your rescue."

Brian arched an eyebrow even as dread grabbed him in a choking grip. "How's that?"

"I've the marshals on another task." He waved a hand. "These gentlemen are going to take you somewhere out of the way."

Adele leaned into Brian. He could feel her body shaking. He wrapped a hand around her waist. He didn't know how, but there had to be a way out of this situation.

Ortega turned and walked away, the squeak of his expensive dress shoes on the linoleum floor shuddered down Brian's spine. Ortega opened the door to the hearing room and stepped inside. Once the door closed behind him, the three men with guns herded Brian and Adele out a side door to a waiting white panel van.

One of the men slid the door open. "Inside."

Brian helped Adele into the van then climbed in behind her. The inside was a cargo area with two sets of manacles welded into the side wall.

"Put those on." The man holding the door open said, his gun trained on them. The other two men jumped into the driver side and the passenger seat.

Brian gave a nod to Adele. For now it would

be best if they did as they were told. He couldn't take out all three of them and keep Adele safe. He clipped the manacles to his wrists and then helped Adele to do the same, though he kept them loose.

The man holding them at gunpoint put a foot into the van, leaned forward and snapped the manacles so tight they bit into Brian's skin, then he snapped Adele's tighter.

"Ow!" she yelped.

Brian bit down on his rage. He wanted to smash his fist into the guy's face for hurting Adele.

The gunman stepped out of the van and replaced his gun in his holster. Then he shoved Brian's Glock and .32 down the storm drain.

Brian was thankful his weapons wouldn't be used against him and Adele, or in a crime.

The gunman straightened and slammed the van's sliding door closed, throwing the back cargo space into inky shadows.

Adele put her head between her knees. He could hear her breathing heavily. No doubt she was fighting off a panic attack.

The engine fired up and the driver threw the van into gear. The van eased away from the curb, rolling down the street and leaving any hope of help behind.

SIXTEEN

Adele battled her emotions. In therapy, she'd learned to name them, which was supposed to help mitigate their power. Fear, anger, anxiety, panic. They all balled in her chest, making breathing difficult. She felt Brian's hand on her knee. That was as far as his manacles would allow him to reach. She shifted so that their hands could meet.

She lifted her eyes to meet his. "I'm so sorry you were caught up in this," she said in a low tone so their captors wouldn't hear.

"Hey now, not your responsibility. We're in this situation because I let my guard down."

Hearing him blame himself brought clarity. "This is all on John." She bared her teeth in a silent growl, wishing she could have slapped John's smug face. "All this time, I had no idea a monster lived behind those bright, pearly teeth and warm brown eyes."

"Only God truly knows what's in the heart of a person," Brian said. "Evil is really good at hiding itself. Evil is really good at making others believe what it wants them to believe."

"You talk as if evil is a living, breathing entity."

"It may be invisible, but I know it's real."

She thought about the life he'd led and the wounds he bore. Thought about her own life and her brushes with evil in the courtroom and out. It stood to reason that on this earth, justice would always bump up against evil. But she knew that Jesus had overcome evil, and that justice may not be served here on earth, but it would be served.

Keeping her voice low, she asked, "How do we get out of this?"

"There's nothing we can do at the moment. We need to wait until we stop."

She took a shuddering breath. "What if they leave us in this van to die?"

Brian squeezed her hand. "We need to stay positive. We can't give up."

No, because giving up meant John and the Overstreet men won. "What do you think John meant when he said he had the US marshals busy doing something else?"

"Who's to say what kind of situation he concocted."

"Well, one thing is for sure. Tomas Garcia's not behind the threats to my life."

"No, he's not, but questioning him gave us a good lead as to who is continuing on with the Garcia cartel. That phone call I received was Sera. She's going to join a task force that will hopefully finally put an end to the cartel."

She sent up a prayer of protection for Sera as well as one for herself and Brian. "At least something good came out of this horrific ordeal. Getting the drugs off the streets is a constant battle."

"A tough battle when there are so many people dependent on them to numb their pain."

Adele's lungs closed. She scrunched up her face as a horrible truth rose within her. She bit down on her tongue to keep the confession bubbling to the surface from exploding outward, but the words would not be stopped. "I tried to numb my pain after Richard assaulted me and I saw that security guard die trying to save me."

She could feel Brian's gaze on her but was thankful for the dim lighting to hide her guilt.

"But you didn't let it destroy you," he said.

"No. I didn't. But only because I had a really good therapist. If I'd have tried to do it on my own—" She shook her head. She'd have failed.

"It's good that you got help. So many people

don't. It's not a sign of weakness. It's a sign of strength to admit you can't do everything on your own."

The conviction in his tone had her asking, "Are you speaking from experience?"

"I am. I battled addiction to pain meds," he said.

She could imagine, remembering the scars covering his body. "How did you beat it?"

"I had a really good support system," he told her. "Just like you do."

"You had the Armstrongs." For that, she was immensely grateful. Her time spent with Victoria had showed her how strong the woman's love and care was for those she helped. And seeing the way Gavin and Jace interacted with Brian, like he was a second son and brother, warmed her heart. The Armstrongs would be devasted, as would her own family, if she and Brian didn't survive this ordeal.

"Yes, the Armstrongs are like family."

She smiled at his echoing her thoughts.

He added, "And you had your loving family."

"True. My parents and sister were my firm foundation." She leaned into him. "It's funny how much we have in common. Yet we are so different."

He murmured, "They say opposites attract."

Her heart bumped against her chest at his words. She swallowed the rising emotions crowding out the anxiety. She wanted to tell this man that she had fallen in love with him. But was she just feeling such intense emotion because of the imminent threat to their lives?

What would happen if they lived through this and then moved on to go about their mundane lives?

She almost laughed. There was nothing mundane about either of their chosen professions. But could the stress of their jobs put too much pressure on the growing love she felt? Did he even feel anything beyond duty and attraction for her?

The questions ricocheted through her mind, but she had no answers. She'd make herself sick with conjecture and theory if she dwelled on the problems of the future. Right now, she needed to stay grounded in the reality that she and Brian were being held hostage in a moving van going to an unknown fate.

The van turned off the smooth highway and onto a jarring, rutted road. With each bump, her teeth rattled and her fear ratcheted upward. Sweat broke out on the back of her neck and trickled down her back. Brian's hand squeezed hers, offering her a comfort that she clung to with all her might.

Finally, after what seemed like an interminably long time, the van drew to a halt. The two men got out of the front. She braced herself for the van door to slide open. But it didn't. Instead, a few minutes later, a pungent odor filled the cargo space of the van. Her heart leapt into her throat with renewed horror.

"Gasoline."

Brian's grim pronouncement sent a fresh wave of panic sweeping over her. She closed her eyes tight and prayed with fervent urgency for salvation.

Brian tried desperately not to let his rising fear overwhelm him. He didn't want to aggravate Adele's own terror any more by revealing his own. He had to get them out of the situation. He stretched his legs and scooted down as far as he could to see if he could reach the other side of the van. His booted feet were just inches away from the side. He tried to stand but the manacles jerked him back to the floor of the van.

"Adele, I need you."

She lifted her head. "What can I do?"

He shifted uncomfortably, lifting his right foot. "Can you reach my right boot?"

"Maybe." She twisted so she could maneuver enough to grab hold of his bootheel.

"Pull as hard as you can," he told her.

"This is difficult," she said. "I can't get a good grip."

"Do the best you can," he implored.

While she tugged, he bent his knee, trying to draw his foot out from the boot, along with it, the small knife he kept hidden inside. Finally, the boot gave way and the knife slid out and bounced on the bottom of the van's metal floor.

A swoosh of noise had the hairs on Brian's neck rising in alarm. The van erupted into flames. He also heard the sound on another vehicle's engine turning over. Their captors were fleeing the scene.

He couldn't think about the fire. He had to concentrate on freeing Adele. Using his foot, he scooted the knife close enough for him to reach. He used the tip and worked it into the locking mechanism.

Smoke billowed inside the van, making them both cough.

The knife's tip was too broad to fit in the small slot. He growled his frustration.

"Would a bobby pin help?"

His pulse jumped. "You have one?"

"In my front left pocket," she said, and twisted and lifted her hips so she could dig her fingers into the pocket. She removed two bobby pins.

"Bless you," he breathed, taking one from her. "Hang on to the other in case I break this one."

He bent the bobby pin apart. Using the flat end like a shim, he slipped it into the groove with the teeth, shoving it as far as he could. The bobby pin released the hold of the teeth. The handcuff fell away. He did the same to her other cuff. "Get out of the van. Go."

She stared at him through the haze of smoke. "Not without you."

He attempted to do the same to his own manacles, but his hands shook and he dropped the bobby pin. "Adele," he barked, "you need to save yourself."

Tucking the spare bobby pin back in her pocket, she grabbed the fallen one. "Talk me through this."

Flames licked at the inside of the cargo hold. Any second, the gas tank and engine would explode. Tears ran down her face. She wiped away the moisture with the sleeve of her windbreaker.

"Don't let him win," Brian said. "You need to leave."

She looked him in the eye. "We are not going to die. Now, what do I do?"

He was so proud of her. Love for her expanded in his chest. He wanted to tell her but instead he said, "Take the flat end and shove it into the teeth's channel."

She did as he instructed. The cuff unlocked. He took the bobby pin from her and released his other hand. Not wasting a second to praise her, he grabbed her by the hand and scrambled into the front seat, pulling her along with him. He opened the passenger door and tumbled out, drawing her with him. He fell with a thud onto his back, and she landed on his chest. He wrapped his arms around her and rolled her away from the van.

They both scrambled to their hands and knees. The gritty desert dirt bit into his hands as he gulped in fresh air. Heat from the van fire buffeted him. He searched the area, his stomach dropping when he realized they were in the middle of nowhere. Flat desert stretched for miles with only sagebrush and an occasional stand of trees visible in every direction.

He tugged Adele to her feet and pressed her to run with him as far from the van as they could. Rocks and debris stabbed into his socked foot. He hadn't thought to grab his other boot.

The van exploded, the concussion of the

blast sending them both flying forward, landing face-first in the dirt.

Brian flipped onto his backside and stared at the burning vehicle. Large plumes of black smoke rose high in the air. As signals for help went, he couldn't have asked for a better one. He prayed their captors didn't circle back.

The sound of distant sirens drawing closer gave Adele hope that they were going to get to safety. She turned to Brian, taking in his handsome face covered with dirt, grime and dark soot. She could only imagine how she looked. But it didn't matter. Nothing mattered except that they were alive. They'd survived so much in a short period of time. A determined certainty filled her. They could survive the future together. Her heart swelled.

She reached up to tenderly touch his face. "Deputy Brian Forrester, I love you."

His eyes widened. His stunned expression made her heart pound. He opened his mouth and she feared he would protest her declaration.

She held up a hand, staving off his rejection. "I do. I may have once questioned my judgment when it came to romantic relationships, but I know deep in my heart that you are a man I can count on. A man I can love and trust and grow old with." She took in a shuddering breath and pushed out the rest of the words crowding her heart. "I'll understand if you don't feel the same. But I just need you to know that now, and in ten minutes, in ten hours, ten days, ten years from now, I will still love you."

His gaze softened and his mouth tipped up at the corners.

Encouraged by the look in his eyes, she continued. "I love you and I hope and pray that when we get back to civilization, we can find a way to move forward together."

Brian cupped her face in his big hands. "That was a lot of words."

She laughed. "What can I say? I'm a lawyer at heart."

He chuckled then sobered. His expression turned earnest and adoring. Her heart skipped several beats.

"I love you, too, Judge Adele Weston. For here, for now, forever."

Her throat clogged with joy. She managed to ask, "You're not afraid?"

"Of course, I'm afraid," he said. "But as a wise woman once told me, if you don't risk your heart, you will never know what is possible."

A fresh wave of love filled Adele to overflowing. "You know, if you tell my mom that I told you what she said, she's going to be so proud of herself."

"She should be proud of herself, because she produced a beautiful, brave, stubborn and resilient daughter whom I couldn't be prouder of. I hope that one day, you will do me the honor of becoming my wife."

Delight exploded in her chest. He was asking her for the ultimate commitment. She didn't hesitate. She drew him in close for a kiss. He tasted of dirt and man and hope for a bright future.

As the sirens drew closer and emergency vehicles came to a halt, spraying up dirt around them, Brian broke the kiss.

"Is that a yes?" he asked.

"Yes." She laughed, feeling more carefree than she had in fifteen years.

Brian wasn't about to leave Adele's side. They rode together in an ambulance to the hospital and sat side by side in the exam room as the doctors checked them over, making sure their lungs were clear and cleaning their superficial wounds.

The only time he left her side was when they

both were given an opportunity to shower and change into fresh clothes.

And now they stood in front of the hearing room.

Jace and Gavin stood beside them.

"The senator is still inside," Gavin told them.

As soon as Gavin realized they'd been sent on a wild-goose chase tracking down a fictional man who claimed to be responsible for hiring the Overstreet brothers to kill Adele, he'd high-tailed it back to the city. Then hearing of the ordeal Brian and Adele had suffered, he'd put the federal building on lockdown and rounded up the senator's henchmen. Brian was in awe of his boss and so grateful.

But Brian wanted Adele to be the one to confront the senator and Overstreet. This situation was the only thing from the past that could mar their future. She needed closure.

With a nod from Adele, Brian opened the door to the hearing room and gestured for her to enter the large open space ahead of him. There was a dais where the parole board members sat. There were two tables facing the board.

Ortega sputtered when he saw them. "What are you doing here?"

"Senator, you are under arrest for attempted murder," Brian took great satisfaction saying as he strode forward and cuffed the senator's hands behind his back.

The parole board members murmured surprise.

"You can't do this," Ortega espoused. "I'm a United States' senator. I'll have your badge for this"

Marshal Gavin Armstrong stepped up into the senator's face. "You will be stripped of any power and your title."

Brian handed off the senator to Gavin, who escorted the man out, then focused his gaze on Adele, who stood in front of the parole board.

"I'm Adele Weston," she said in a clear, strong voice. "Richard Overstreet assaulted me and killed the man who tried to help me."

She turned to face her attacker.

Brian got his first good look at Richard Overstreet. The man's thin, hunched shoulders and downcast stare was meant to evoke empathy. But the dark eyes that stared at Adele from a hooded gaze glittered with a malice that matched his father's. Richard Overstreet truly was Senator John Ortega's son.

"You robbed me of so much," Adele said. "No more. You have no power over me or my life. And I will make sure you never hurt anyone else again." She turned back to the parole board. "Senator Ortega is Richard Overstreet's father. He orchestrated this parole hearing. I implore this board to deny parole."

"Thank you, Judge Weston, for your input. We will take it under advisement." The spokesperson for the parole board raised the gavel and banged it. "We are in recess."

Brian held his hand out to Adele. With a smile, she threaded her fingers through his and together they walked out of the hearing room without a backward glance.

"Do you want to wait and hear the parole board's decision?"

She shook her head. "He's no longer my burden to bear."

They walked out into the February sunshine, hand in hand. Then they climbed into a waiting SUV. Conlan was driving and Scout was sitting in the passenger seat, secured by a harness attached to the headrest to keep him safe. The dog howled with joy at seeing Adele. She reached forward to greet him and let him lick her face.

"Where are we going?" Conlan asked.

"To the judge's home," Brian said.

"Do you hear that Scout?" Adele said. "We're going home. And we'll be seeing Brian again soon." She grinned at Brian.

He grinned back as love expanded in his chest. He couldn't be happier to be included in her life.

The ding of an incoming text diverted Brian's attention. He pulled his phone out to check. He smiled to see the message from Jace.

Parole denied.

Brian tucked the phone back in his pocket and pulled Adele close, savoring the moment as they raced toward their future.

Together.

* * * * *

If you enjoyed this story, please look for these other books by Terri Reed:

Forced to Flee
Secret Sabotage
Christmas Protection Detail

Dear Reader,

It's always a joy to visit with characters from a previous book and give secondary characters their own story. In *Forced to Hide*, we are re-introduced to US deputy marshal Brian Forrester. I had fun writing about him in *Forced to Flee* and then exploring more about this interesting man.

When I came up with the idea for this novel, I started with a judge under attack. I didn't know why or by whom. I decided to make it a female judge and then it seemed right to pair her with Brian, after all, part of the US marshals' job is to protect judges. Letting them have a bit of a history, and then seeing where the story took them, was a roller-coaster ride.

Judge Adele Weston had a traumatic past that kept her from finding love. As she let down her guard and let Brian in, we learned how she coped, and we got to watch her grow through her anxiety. I love giving my characters a strong ending and hope for a bright future. I hope you agree that Brian and Adele were a good match and worked well together under pressure.

I hope to bring you more books with the US

marshals, but coming up next from me will be Book 3 of a new continuity series from Love Inspired Suspense. This story will feature K-9s and their handlers protecting the beautiful forests of Washington State.

Until we meet again, may God bless you greatly,

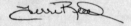

Get 4 FREE REWARDS!

We'll send you 2 FREE Books plus 2 FREE Mystery Gifts.

FREE
Value Over
$20

Both the **Harlequin® Special Edition** and **Harlequin® Heartwarming™** series feature compelling novels filled with stories of love and strength where the bonds of friendship, family and community unite.

THE 2022 LOVE INSPIRED CHRISTMAS COLLECTION

Buy 3 and get 1 FREE!

May all that is beautiful, meaningful and brings you joy be yours this holiday season…including this fun-filled collection featuring 24 Christmas stories. From tender holiday romances to Christmas Eve suspense, this collection has it all.

YES! Please send me the **2022 LOVE INSPIRED CHRISTMAS COLLECTION** in Larger Print! This collection begins with **ONE FREE** book and **2 FREE** gifts in the first shipment. Along with my FREE book, I'll get another 3 Larger Print books! If I do not cancel, I will continue to receive four books a month for five more months. Each shipment will contain another FREE gift. I'll pay just $23.97 U.S./$26.97 CAN., plus $1.99 U.S./$4.99 CAN. for shipping and handling per shipment.* I understand that accepting the free books and gifts places me under no obligation to buy anything. I can always return a shipment and cancel at any time. My free books and gifts are mine to keep no matter what I decide.

☐ 298 HCK 0958   ☐ 498 HCK 0958

Name (please print)

Address   Apt. #

City   State/Province   Zip/Postal Code

Mail to the **Harlequin Reader Service:**
IN U.S.A.: P.O. Box 1341, Buffalo, NY 14240-8531
IN CANADA: P.O. Box 603, Fort Erie, ON L2A 5X3

XMASL2022